YOU DON'T KNOW LOVE
UNTIL YOU'VE BEEN KISSED.

Cheryl Crawford relished the initial seconds of awareness when her husband, Justin, invaded her personal space, crowding her air with his distinguished presence, until every breath that filled her lungs was of him. He possessed a power over her that had her nose so wide open she couldn't even speak of it in the hushed covenant of privacy she and her sisters-in-law shared.

Justin didn't even have to be within feet of her; yards were enough to start her juices flowing and make her forget her perpetual state of want. And want him she did, with the bleak-eyed focus of a junky.

BOOK YOUR PLACE ON OUR WEBSITE AND MAKE THE READING CONNECTION!

We've created a customized website just for our very special readers, where you can get the inside scoop on everything that's going on with Zebra, Pinnacle and Kensington books.

When you come online, you'll have the exciting opportunity to:

- View covers of upcoming books
- Read sample chapters
- Learn about our future publishing schedule (listed by publication month *and author*)
- Find out when your favorite authors will be visiting a city near you
- Search for and order backlist books from our online catalog
- Check out author bios and background information
- Send e-mail to your favorite authors
- Meet the Kensington staff online
- Join us in weekly chats with authors, readers and other guests
- Get writing guidelines
- AND MUCH MORE!

**Visit our website at
http://www.kensingtonbooks.com**

KISSED

Carmen Green

DAFINA BOOKS
Kensington Publishing Corp.
http://www.kensingtonbooks.com

DAFINA BOOKS are published by

Kensington Publishing Corp.
850 Third Avenue
New York, NY 10022

All Kensington titles, imprints and distributed lines are available at special quantity discounts for bulk purchases for sales
promotions, premiums, fund-raising, educational or institu-
tional use.

Special book excerpts or customized printings can also be created to fit specific needs. For details, write or phone the office
of the Kensington Special Sales Manager: Kensington Publishing Corp., 850 Third Avenue, New York, NY 10022. Attn.
Special Sales Department. Phone: 1-800-221-2647.

Dafina Books and the Dafina logo Reg. U.S. Pat. & TM Off.

First Printing: November 2004
10 9 8 7 6 5 4 3 2 1

Printed in the United States of America

*To my mom, Mildred McCray,
you are the source of inspiration and hope.
I'm so thankful that you're my mother and
every day I'm blessed by your love.*

One

Cheryl Crawford relished the initial seconds of awareness when her husband, Justin, invaded her personal space, crowding her air with his distinguished presence, until every breath that filled her lungs was of him. He possessed a power over her that had her nose so wide open she couldn't even speak of it in the hushed covenant of privacy she and her sisters-in-law shared.

They attributed her silence to years of cultivated refinement; after all, she'd been with him more than half her life. But they didn't know how much she wanted, no, needed him in her life. Apart from her relationship with the Almighty, he was her everything.

Justin didn't even have to be within feet of her; yards were enough to start her juices flowing and make her forget her perpetual state of want. And want him she did, with the bleak-eyed focus of a junky.

There was only one way to sate her blinding desire. It was the definitive conclusion that had ended thousands of times in the exact same manner: with her fetal-like, hoarding the evaporating thrill of having just experienced a simultaneous burst of what for her was synonymous only with him.

He was *Zing*.

That mystical magnetic power that raided her body like the FBI on a meth lab, until there was nothing left on her lips but "*Ah*."

Zing.

The fire that burned from his gray-eyed gaze would slap her on the ass across a crowded room and make her scurry for the confines of a bedroom, bathroom, closet, or God help her, a balcony.

Zing.

Damn him.

He had it and he knew how to use it. Like P. Diddy to rap, a baby to a full breast, all he had to do was reach out a finger, quirk one full brow, lick his lips, or crook up the corner of his mouth and she was his.

As they stood inside the Pacific Mausoleum in Ecuador, Cheryl slipped from the crowd admiring him and went outside into the evening spring air.

"You are exactly as I'd pictured. Absolutely luscious."

She pivoted on her recent birthday presents, three-thousand-dollar René Mancini shoes, and looked at her uninvited suitor.

Chad Brown had worked as Justin's top aide for the past year and had come into his own as a political insider. Cheryl didn't doubt that one day he'd make a formidable opponent, in the boardroom as well as elsewhere. In addition to being smart, he was as handsome and cocky as the tilt of his lips.

Bold wasn't accurate enough to describe a man who'd fall in like with a married woman. Wrong was a better description, but Cheryl stopped short of passing judgment. He was making passes at her, and she hadn't cussed him out for overstepping his bounds.

The truth was, she bore his flirtations in guilty silence because the rare times he'd dared breach the line of propriety with his highly shined Kenneth Coles, she'd been dying for the attention of another man. Her husband. And Justin didn't pay her any mind.

"You should be working," she told Chad, who stood with his hands in his pockets, the single-breasted suit jacket mussed but perfect.

"Even God rested. But then there's Justin."

Cheryl wasn't going there. Not with a man she could see herself getting to know if they'd met in another lifetime.

"I'm proud of my husband," Cheryl informed him. "You should be more respectful of your boss."

She gathered the train of the beautiful lavender Vera Wang dress and stepped lightly down the stairs.

"Lies from a beautiful woman's lips are poison in the veins of those who care about them."

Heat flushed Cheryl's face. "Why would I lie? My husband *is* working hard for all of us."

"Then why are you out here? Lonely?" He walked down the stairs deliberately. "Tired of being so beautiful, and dutiful, and alone?"

He closed the distance between them and Cheryl wouldn't back away. Chad kept erasing the symbolic line of propriety, until she knew she'd have to be seriously direct, except he was right. She almost couldn't refute his assessment. "You're out of line," she said. "And I'm married."

"Happy—"

"Has nothing to do with you."

Cheryl turned and before she could fully extend her arm, the car she'd hired to take her home had been signaled by Chad.

"How did you know?" she said into the balmy stillness.

"You're royalty," he said as if she should have known, and opened the car door and extended his hand. "It's my job to know just about everything."

She considered what the taxi driver might think, but knew it would get around town if she refused to accept Chad's hand of assistance. She hated the direction of her thoughts. She was tired of being a public figure's wife. Tired of caring what everyone else thought. For once she wanted to sit back and just be. She wanted her husband to do the same.

Chad held the door and she slid into the cool vehicle. Before the driver could get back into the car, Chad glanced at him. "*Uno momento, señor.*"

The man nodded and stepped away.

Chad crouched down until they were eye level. "If he doesn't know how exquisite you are, he may as well let you be with someone who'll never forget. Your mouth is—damn." He sighed as his gaze strolled leisurely over her MAC-glammed lips. "When was the last time you were kissed?"

Before Cheryl could help herself, she licked her lips. Chad swore again, softly. He fingered the silk of her floor-length skirt. "Good night, Mrs. Crawford."

Cheryl waited until the driver had hit the main road before she breathed. Chad was playing with her head. So how could he have known the depth of her insecurities?

She loved Justin to the very core of her soul. And up until now, she'd have done anything for him. Yet, despite her decision to complete the interview process for the teaching job at the University of South Africa, a decision that wouldn't be popular with her husband, she still yearned for his touch.

Cheryl had to remind herself that sex wasn't everything. She had to tell herself that the magnitude of her discontent was at a point where she had to follow her dreams or succumb once and for all to "the life."

Beacons of light from the shore reflected off the dazzling Pacific, strong the way she was supposed to be, and Cheryl silently praised herself for taking a stand in her own behalf.

She wouldn't be one of those women in the relationship section of *Jet* magazine, married for sixty years, but not a smile to be found on her or her groom. Those couples weren't fooling anyone. Each was waiting for the other to die before they would either live it up or live in peace.

Hell no, she thought.

That wouldn't be her.

"*Casa, por favor,*" she said. A tinge of the loneliness that had taken root in her heart fell from her lips with the words.

Justin commanded respect and got results. He was revered and quoted, articulate and charismatic. When sought, he went, and wherever he went success followed.

He'd conquered her long ago. Were it not for the death grip of assuredness that she was doing the right thing, she would be at his side right now, trying to coax him out of schmoozing and into a romp in bed with her, the one woman who'd trusted him implicitly with her body and heart.

They'd done it all, in every way imaginable, but he still had that power of surprise and took her to new heights regularly.

Last night had been rough, raw, aggressive, and powerful. He'd taken hold of her foot, pulled her quivering body to him, and plunged. She'd cried out his name to the melody of a crashing orgasm, and she was sure nothing in life could get sweeter than that.

"Señor," she said, breathless. "Take me back."

Through the rearview mirror, he eyed her curiously and obeyed. Two-thirds into a three-point turn, her mind and body battled until desperation shoved desire against the glass ceiling of her life and forced her to look.

At night Justin knew how to coax responses from her body she didn't know she possessed. Out of bed, he barely knew she existed.

"Stop," she cried in Spanish. "Please, take me home."

"Señora?" The driver stopped in the middle of the road, causing cars to careen around them, horns blaring.

The metaphor of the swiveling vehicles mirrored her life too closely.

"When it is safe, please turn around and take me home. A nice tip for you. Double," she said, and pulled the money from her bag.

The cash was enough to suspend his doubt about her sanity, yet he wasted no time in getting her to her door and out of his car.

To his credit he waited until she was inside before peeling off the majestic driveway of her stately home. The tire marks would anger Juan, the property manager. He'd question the staff until the culprit confessed. She'd have to speak with him in the morning before he fired everyone.

Cheryl took the winding staircase up to the bedroom and opened the French doors. She ignored the huge bed and the memories it evoked, stopped at her desk, and withdrew a sheet of stationery.

In the past, expressing herself verbally hadn't worked. Maybe the written word would capture his attention.

Cheryl sank down, kicked the train of her dress aside, and let the pen touch the paper. The words began to flow.

"My darling Justin,
I love you so much it hurts me to write this, but it's time you knew how I felt. I miss us. I miss our private time together, the long walks in the park and

the passionate kisses we used to share under Atlanta's bright sun. I miss the person you were before you became an ambassador three years ago. Before the will of the people became more of a priority than our commitment to each other. Please resign, Justin, and go with me so that I can teach in Africa as we agreed, and in the process I believe we can find our way back to each other. I'm willing to start over. Let's recapture our love with one intimate kiss under the exotic sky.

I love you with all my heart.

Cheryl

Cheryl released the pen, suddenly tired. Hopefully Justin would listen.

But what if he didn't?

Two

Sharply dressed men and women bathed in White Diamonds perfume had filled the ballroom of the Pacific Mausoleum to honor University President Carlos Ramirez, and the college-level Accelerated Learning Program Justin had founded. Justin should have been working his guests, but all he noticed was the retreating back of his wife, Cheryl.

Where was she going?

Maybe she did have an ulcer, he begrudgingly conceded. She'd certainly complained enough for the past few weeks about having an upset stomach. She hadn't wanted to see a doctor, so he'd thought she was fine. Only, her disposition hadn't improved.

Once he'd made the mistake of suggesting it was PMS. To say she'd gone off on him would be an understatement. Even now, the memory of her wrath rocked him onto his heels. Cheryl wasn't given to tantrums. That's why he'd endured that one, but her behavior had certainly raised concern. When women in her position of public prominence lost control, something serious and private was usually the cause.

He'd turned detective and asked Mirta, the maid, if his wife was into something he should know about. She'd surprised him and rolled her neck, reminiscent of every ticked-off black woman he'd ever known. She'd said no, but he felt the unspoken "hell" as though she'd spat it at him.

She'd taken her dust cloth, slapped it on the cherry-wood sofa table, and slammed out of the room as if he'd turned their home into a crack house.

He had no choice but to take matters into his own hands. He'd never violated Cheryl's personal privacy before, but her behavior made everything fair game.

The thirty-by-thirty-foot closet, cooler than the bedroom by fifteen degrees, was daunting in its sophisticated splendor. Facing him was a wall of slender Italian glass drawers that reminded him of safety deposit boxes. He hadn't known there were so many until he'd embarked upon the task of inspecting each one.

The discoveries he'd made about Cheryl had him less sure she was the woman he had married than a stranger that had taken her place.

Gone were the predictable cotton underwear, replaced by barely-there triangles and satin-cupped bras his fingers slowed over.

The aroma of her perfume, a fragrance he'd not known her to wear, stirred his sex and invaded his senses until he'd had to take a step back, ashamed. He'd come here for one thing and it wasn't to smell his wife's underwear.

In a hurry to leave, he stopped at her medicine

chest. The cabinet sat empty of prescription bottles, but she had makeup tubes, bottles, jars, and things that looked suspiciously like syringes filled with grainy goop that dried on his fingers.

Why did Cheryl have all this junk?

She possessed a natural beauty. Too much makeup, in his opinion, was for women who had something to hide.

Well, she wasn't a drug user, and for that he was grateful. He'd left her private sanctum and closed the door soundly behind him.

Cheryl was just changing.

So he'd been quiet about her withdrawn demeanor, figuring she'd speak her piece eventually. She never had, and on a special occasion like tonight, her behavior affected him.

As she disappeared, he made no move to follow her. She'd tell him if she needed him. But even as he turned to look at the guests who'd come out in support of Ramirez, and indirectly him, Justin felt as if they were being cheated.

He and Cheryl were a power couple, and they were expected to mingle and spread goodwill.

Although no money would change hands tonight, attendance at this event was an implied donation. Checks would flow into his office before week's end. By the guests' happy expressions, their generosity would likely reach half a million dollars.

"Crawford, I didn't expect you to be at something so charitable. These highfalutin back-pattin' dinners have always been too lowbrow for you, except when you're the honoree or it's for African-American kids."

Solomon Grossman, ambassador to Puerto

Rico, heckled him, his nasal voice engorged with allergens and a bad sinus operation.

Justin's assistant and protégé, Chadwick Brown, arrived too late to steer the older man from Justin's path. Justin lightly flicked his wrist and Chad and Herb, his second assistant, stopped five feet away but close enough if needed. One of them would have to drive Grossman to his hotel anyway.

"You know better, Gross," Justin responded, unfazed. "These kids have become very important to me. They represent the future of Ecuador."

Justin had brought the Accelerated Learning Program to Ecuador. Modeled after the state of Georgia's HOPE Scholarship, he'd taken the program one step further. The recipients of this four-year scholarship agreed to give back one year of service for every year of free tuition. Last year ten students had received the scholarship, and this year, fifteen. In just three short years, Ecuador would begin to reap the benefit this program had been created for.

Grossman wanted to do more than emulate Justin's success. He wanted Justin's benefactors, and Justin wasn't going to allow the desperate man to leave this country with a dollar that was earmarked for his students.

"How is Eleanor?" Justin asked.

"Lots of bad days, but as well as can be expected." Grossman's tongue sought the tart taste of Chablis as it skated nervously across his lips. Justin knew an alcoholic when he saw one. A passing waiter answered the silent call. He drank deeply. "Cancer is a bitch."

Justin nodded, thinking Eleanor had recently improved. He frowned at the misinformation. He turned to give Cheryl the eye, but she was still MIA. "I'm sorry. I thought she'd had some better days."

"A relapse." Grossman grew sadder.

Justin longed for Cheryl. She had a way of steering him away from conversational land mines and giving him the right words. How could he be expected to remember everything about everybody? Cheryl's job was to make him look informed and caring.

Annoyance flashed through him. She'd have to figure out what the hell was wrong with her stomach another day.

"Excuse me. I've got to see about my wife."

"Obviously Cheryl's visit last week was what Eleanor needed. She took her into the gardens. I heard them laughing." Solomon looked wistful as Justin stayed frozen in place. "Even I haven't done that. You've got one special lady."

"Yes. Special." Justin checked his embarrassment. What the hell had Cheryl been doing in Puerto Rico?

She'd said she'd gone to their home in Atlanta to see about their son who'd caught a cold. The whole trip had seemed foolish as far as he was concerned. Jett was a freshman at Georgia Tech, but Cheryl had been adamant.

Yet now that he thought about it, in the past for her a visit to Atlanta meant shopping and a flurry of phone calls between Cheryl and the other Crawford wives.

The phones had been quiet. His wife, still sullen.

Cheryl had lied to him.

"Where is Cheryl? I wanted to thank her personally," Grossman said and drank, the empty glass disappointing him. His gaze wandered.

"She stepped out a moment ago. A spring cold. You know how those can sneak up on you. I'll pass along your thanks." And demand an explanation about her secret life. Was she cheating on him? She couldn't be. He was happy, so why the hell wasn't she?

Tonight he'd confront her in the only place he could still elicit more than a monosyllabic response. In bed.

"I'd better mingle with the checkbooks—guests," Grossman rephrased.

A subtle nod to his second aide, Herb, and Solomon was deeply engaged in a conversation on the significance of imports and exports to Puerto Rico, and the impact they had on their future society. Justin slid away as Chad sidled over.

"Have you heard about Senator Dan North?"

"Have you seen my wife?"

Both spoke at once but Chad answered first. "She left in a private car a half hour ago." His bookish face carried the look of a concerned assistant who didn't want to infringe upon his boss's privacy.

"That's right," Justin responded, as if he'd known she was leaving. "What's up with Dan?"

"This evening he had a fatal heart attack."

Sadness engulfed him. While at Emory Law School, they'd been best friends, but as their political aspirations had grown, their friendship had drifted apart.

"Send our condolences, first thing." He stopped when he realized Cheryl wasn't with him. "Chad, make a note for Cheryl to send condolences to Lea and Sam. Sam's at Tech with my son Jett. A call to Jett, too. What a loss."

"Maura's still at the office. She can send the note along with condolence flowers, and leave the call for Cheryl, uh, Mrs. Crawford?"

Justin took note of the verbal adjustment. She'd been Mrs. Crawford for six months and now she was Cheryl?

What the hell was going on right under his nose?

He didn't look away from Chad. "I prefer Mrs. Crawford send the notes. That leaves Maura to handle other important business."

"Yes, sir." Justin didn't read fear in Chad's eyes, but noted that the hint of challenge took an extra few seconds to dissipate. "No disrespect intended. I apologize."

Justin relaxed his shoulders. "Accepted."

"For your loss," Chad interjected, flatly. "I know you and Senator North go all the way back to law school."

He's young, Justin thought. Too young to understand real relationships, not having had a serious girlfriend ever since he'd joined the team a year ago.

He also didn't realize that dancing on Justin's toes could end his career. But Justin understood raw talent. And it was better to have Chad on his side than not.

"Keep your eye on the ball, Chad. That's where the action is."

"Right, sir." Each retreated to a neutral corner for a few seconds. "An important seat is now open in the Senate. The Democratic Party will probably throw their support behind Congressman Hilliard Brandt, but he's had some sobriety difficulties in the past."

"Who hasn't?" With the outing of celebrities like Limbaugh, struggling with addiction was now accepted in society.

"The party will have a short list by dawn," Justin informed him. "Let's say good night to these fine folks and get ready for tomorrow."

Chad left, but Justin's mind was stuck on the subject of North's passing. He toyed with his cell phone, wanting to call Lea. Even after all this time, he still thought fondly of the woman who'd taken him on his first trip around a woman's body. They'd dated in college, and then he'd met Cheryl and his life had changed forever.

Now Lea's husband was dead.

Justin wanted to talk to her, make sure she was okay, but he didn't have her number.

Inspiration hit and he dialed directory assistance. "Georgia. Atlanta. Lea North," he said to the prompts.

"You've requested a number that is unlisted."

Of course. She was a senator's wife.

He snapped the phone shut. Cheryl would have their private number in her PDA.

Justin eased back into the ballroom and said good-bye to the guests, although the wife of a popular mayor made her wishes for a private get-together known. He finessed his way out of the situation, his thoughts gravitating back to his wife.

Cheryl had never told him no. In his mind, shopping in a different store didn't mean better merchandise.

Even with Grossman's news of Cheryl's visit dogging him, he still wanted her.

He hurried to his car and made it home in fifteen minutes.

As the tires of his Lexus met the driveway, he marveled at the view of white lights reflecting off nineteenth-century marble pillars.

There were definite perks to being an ambassador, but before he could consider his appointment a success, he had to close this deal he'd been babysitting for ten months.

The environmental study between the U.S. and Ecuador would bring a two-billion-dollar grant into the Ecuadorian economy over the next ten years. If the deal closed.

They'd just entered into the final phase, and Justin vowed that nothing would get in the way.

Inside the quiet mansion, he stopped in his office and as he removed his tie, Justin pulled a beer from the refrigerator and clicked on his computer to get his messages.

Two were from Maura, reminding him of his brother Eric's and his mother's birthdays in ten days. The third voice made him swallow.

"Ambassador Crawford, this is Senator Tommy Ahern," he drawled, southern style. "Call me, no matter the hour."

Justin stopped long enough to pull off his suit

jacket and dialed. "Tom, Justin Crawford. Is it too late to call?"

"Not a problem. How was your fund-raiser?"

"Successful." Ahern had eyes everywhere.

"A good and smart answer," Tommy complimented, sounding awake despite the time difference on the east coast. "We lost a fine senator in Dan North, but I'll cut to the chase here, Justin. Several friends of Georgia expressed high interest in you to replace Senator North."

"Me?" Justin didn't have the fortitude to sound as shocked as he felt. "Why?"

"Now isn't the time to be modest. You're more than qualified." Tommy's voice dropped. "I'm gonna be frank with you. You have a real shot. Only thing can stop this train is you. Do you have any extracurricular business that would prevent the continuation of this conversation?"

"No. None."

"Good." Ahern sounded extremely pleased. "Any thoughts?"

"Dan just died, Tommy. I've hardly had time to digest that." On principle, Justin never evaded questions. But he needed time to figure out a response. "I need twenty-four hours."

"Ten years ago, I'd have said the same thing. Only we don't have the luxury of time. Nine o'clock tomorrow morning I've scheduled a teleconference and expect to hear your thoughts. I know you were friends with Dan and Lea. Sabrina and I extend our heartfelt sympathy. Think things over t'night. We'll talk first thing tomorrow."

Justin hung up, stunned.

The possibility of a Senate seat roared through

him like lightning. The little boy in him rejoiced. He had been handpicked by Georgia's elite. He could attain his third most ambitious goal in life. The Oval Office was possibly two steps away.

Senator. It sounded sweet to his ears.

Yet a war waged. The people of Ecuador needed him to fulfill his promise and bring that grant home. But he could affect a lot of lives as a senator, not just in his home state, but in the country. He needed to talk to someone. Bounce ideas. He almost dialed his father, but he'd scare his mother by calling so late.

Cheryl. She was probably asleep.

He'd wake her up. They needed to clear the air anyway. His life was changing. And hers would, too.

When he rounded his desk, a fuchsia-colored envelope lay on the chair, his wife's handwriting looped across the top in dark purple ink.

He pulled the stationery out of the envelope and read.

Dan's death shocked him, but this letter sent a whole different level of emotions through him. Angrily, he slammed it on the desk.

Cheryl was miserable because of him?

He provided the luxury she soaked in every day. The food, the lifestyle, the secret trips to Puerto Rico!

If she thought he was going to take responsibility for her unhappiness, then she didn't know him.

And Cheryl knew him well.

How could she even think of wanting him to

leave politics now? Of course she didn't know about the opportunity . . .

Justin could keep Dan's legacy alive. But he couldn't do that from South Africa.

A night full of conflicting emotions faced him, and he knew of only one way to burn the adrenaline and clear his mind to make decisions that might change the direction of his life.

He took the stairs two at a time, the white carpet absorbing his determined footfalls. He had to see her face. If she'd been with another man, he'd know. If she hadn't, he could forgive the letter, and their lovemaking would take care of the rest. He needed her right now.

The white shirt constricted his wrists and he fumbled with the buttons until they gave way.

The door pushed open, and through the filmy haze of fabric surrounding their bed, he saw her.

Cheryl moved, stunned, then began a slow-motion retreat.

Had she cheated?

He approached, undressing on the way. Her movements were jerky, but not defensive.

"Justin?" Her vulnerable voice reached out and quickened his heartbeat. God, he wanted her.

"Have you slept with another man?"

"No."

Pure, unadulterated relief stormed through him like the army's 112th Battalion.

"You wouldn't ever, would you?"

"No."

His shirt fell away, exposing a six-pack of abs that he worked hard to maintain. "Come here."

Cheryl was as lovely as the day they'd married. They *were* partners. Couldn't she see that?

"My note." Her gaze fell to his aroused state and Justin stretched out over her, his arm by her head, his knee parting her thighs.

He met resistance. Their gazes locked. "We'll deal with it."

Relief and trust flooded her ebony eyes and confirmed what he'd known since the day they met. They'd always be together.

He slid his hand under the satiny top and sought final confirmation of her desire for him. "Open for me."

"Promise? We'll talk tomorrow?"

It took him a second to register that Cheryl was still talking about her note.

"I promise." Justin found her elevator button to bliss and pushed.

She gave way to him, and for the next two hours he reminded her of why they were supposed to be.

Three

For the second day in a row, Cheryl awoke flat on her back, her nipples budded to the morning breeze, the rest of her body relaxed as it usually was after great sex. She sat up, annoyed.

Why had she let Justin touch her again?

He had a way of making her mind and body turn to mush. The thought of life without him brought tears to her eyes, yet she was almost without him now. Regaining something only one person thought was lost was like rolling a boulder uphill.

Instead of mulling further, she hurried through her shower and then sat at her dressing table where she bathed her moist skin in vanilla cream lotion. Her thighs were still sensitive from their robust lovemaking. The memory of Justin's hands and face on them sent a waterfall of tingles up and down her legs.

He'd done everything to please her. Pulled tricks from his invisible bag and had invented some she'd never known.

She damned herself because when she looked into the mirror, she confronted the image of a woman who was sexually pleased and emotionally unsettled.

Why did I fall for his false assurances?

Justin's actions spoke louder than any words he could say. He appeared to have been able to reprogram her with sex and more sex.

Cheryl inhaled deeply as she pulled on her satin bra and lace boy-cut panties. Justin may have been smart, but she wasn't a fool.

Inside the desk drawer she found the letter she'd been holding to share with Justin from the University of South Africa. She'd had it for two weeks, hoping for the right opportunity to share it with him, but now her time was nearly up.

She had to respond or they would choose someone else.

Cheryl reached for shorts, but pulled down a dress befitting her status. Holding it against her body, she looked at the nicely woven cotton, but moved deeper into the closet for her smaller clothes. Losing thirty pounds had its benefits and pitfalls.

She dropped the dress into the bag designated for charity and then selected her shoes and put on her makeup.

She tried to devise a plan to confront Justin and couldn't. Even singing Diana Ross's "Ain't No Mountain High Enough" wasn't enough.

Should she march into his office and demand they talk? What if he didn't say anything she wanted to hear? What if he kept making love to her every night and ignoring her during the day?

Before she let her self-confidence become mud

under her shoes, Cheryl dialed her sister-in-law, Keisha, and waited for the ringing to stop.

"Hello?" Julian said.

"Hey," Cheryl said to Justin's oldest brother. "What are you doing home?"

"Kids need to go to the dentist. That's not my thing. I'm waiting for the washer repairman."

Cheryl smiled. Keisha had obviously banned him from fixing things around the house. "Nick not available to come over?"

Colonel Nick Crawford, USMC, was the brother the entire family looked to when something was broken. Between him and his bounty-hunter wife, they took care of everything.

"Jade went into labor this morning. Justin didn't tell you?"

Cheryl kept her disappointment locked in her throat. "No, but he's been in a meeting all morning," she said, her voice softer than she wanted it to be.

Nick and Jade's baby coming was a big deal. How could he not mention it? "He'll probably tell me at lunch." The lie slipped from her lips and Cheryl bit her tongue. Lying to herself had gotten her to this point now. She had to stop covering for her empty marriage.

"Where's Keisha?" she asked.

"Upstairs, trying to help the twins find their cheerleading outfits. They've got dentist appointments later. How are you, baby girl?"

"Good," she said brightly. "Ecuador is exceptionally beautiful this spring."

The silence between them grew, and Cheryl couldn't think of anything else to fill it. She couldn't share her troubles with Julian. The Crawfords were such a close family that they could give lessons to a cult. If she confided her concerns in Julian, there would be five brothers on her doorstep before dinner. She'd always admired their loyalty to each other, but she wanted to regain her marital footing without the help of the entire clan.

"Well, you sound good." Julian sounded distracted. "I'll get Keisha. Bye, darlin'."

"Bye, Julian. Love you."

"You too, baby girl."

The clatter and chatter in the background reminded Cheryl to call Jett. She missed him and his noisy friends. The clothes strewn about, the look in her son's eyes when she asked him to cut the grass. All ten acres.

"Hello?" Breathless, Keisha's voice filled her ear.

All the pretense Cheryl had maintained with Julian was gone. "I'm a chicken. I'm up in the room and I have to tell him about the job today. If I don't mail off the letter, they might select someone else."

"Why did you wait so long?"

Cheryl laughed a little. "I don't know." She closed her eyes on the austere beauty of her room. It was so boring. "I'm afraid of what he'll say."

"What are you scared of? You have a right to work in the career you chose. Besides, I thought you two had agreed eons ago."

Keisha's way of sounding firm and compassionate at the same time prodded Cheryl into confiding, "I'm afraid of what he might say. South Africa is so far away. What will he do all day?"

"What do *you* do all day?"

"I manage this house, the staff, this family. I make sure he's taken care of—" Cheryl halted and inhaled deeply and let the breath out slowly. "Point taken. He can find ways to take care of us too. But—"

"Cheryl, can you continue as you have been?"

"No."

"Then you have your answer. You're a strong woman. Show him who you really are. Until he comes around to your way of thinking, stop being so available. Stop making him so happy. Show him what it feels like to be you. Keep your eyes off that bed, forget how he makes you feel each time you're in the sack, and get your husband back! I've got to run. The twins are late, and I have a date at the spa. See you tomorrow?"

"For what?"

"The funeral." Keisha's voiced dropped. "Don't start getting forgetful when it's important. Dan and Lea were Justin's good friends."

"I know. I'm so sorry."

"It's okay. Really," Keisha said, but Cheryl knew better.

She inserted the phone's earpiece and searched her jewelry tower for her twelfth-anniversary Tiffany's necklace and bracelet. Gliding on the cool platinum, she felt her pulse slow.

Why not look pretty? The jewelry made a statement. It shouted like her pastor in her hometown of Columbus used to. *I'm here. Pay attention to* me. When Justin had given it to her and told her his thinking behind it, they'd shared a big laugh and made love all night. He was her everything. But what would happen when she stepped out on change?

"Julian and Michael are attending the funeral as well as Pop and Ma Vivian," Keisha said.

"I guess I forgot about it because I don't want to go. But it's part of my duties."

"I'll be glad when you're not an ambassador's wife. It's got to be hell being *on* all the time. Doing what others want, when they want. Regardless of how you feel."

"I don't mean to sound ungrateful, but when the eyes of the country are on you, it's hard to be normal. Even with you being six feet tall, you blend in better than me. I absolutely hate it."

"Did you ever imagine it would be this way?"

"Not ever. I imagined us doing actual work— not meetings, but being in the trenches with the people and helping them that way. I was so naive. I didn't realize it took dozens of meetings to even have a trench."

"Yeah," Keisha agreed. "I served on the board of directors for the kids' club and it was insane. People argue just to hear themselves talk."

"I want to teach girls to be leaders, not doormats, and if they choose to be moms and housewives, then great. But they need a happy medium so that they don't lose themselves or their husbands in the process."

"You sound like you're running for political office. Do your thing, sister. Look, I'd better get going. See you tomorrow. Love ya," Keisha said before hanging up.

"Love you, too." Cheryl hung up the phone and gave herself the once-over. Slim again for the first time in her thirties, she was proud of the image she saw.

She cut her eyes away from their king-size bed, and tabled the memories of his hands on her breasts followed by his lips . . . and at the door of their room, she drew her shoulders back and headed downstairs to confront her man.

Four

"You look amazing."

Chad's look of masculine appreciation glittered like black diamonds from his eyes. Guilt filled her because her heart actually leaped at the compliment. "I've never seen a more beautiful woman, Cheryl."

"Where's Justin?" She tried to regain a more level footing.

"He can't be disturbed. He's on a conference call with Tommy Ahern."

Cheryl walked to the door, knocked softly, and went into her husband's office. The inner sanctum expressed Justin to a tee. Clean, concise lines, grays and blues. She motioned hello with her envelope and Justin sat up in his chair. "Just a minute, Tommy. I'm going to put you on hold." He looked at her with the most sexy eyes she'd ever seen. Only they were looking at her as if she were a foreign object. "Cheryl, I'm in the middle of an important call."

"I know but I needed to talk to you. Will you be long?"

"I'm not sure. Has something come up with the family?"

Outrage inflamed her. "No, but we didn't finish our conversation."

"Okay," he said, his face expressionless. "We'll talk, but not right now. Check with Chad and see what I have today."

Cheryl wanted to ask him when she'd been relegated to speaking to him through his assistant. Justin might be busy, but he wasn't God. She hoped he wasn't trying to renege on his word.

She tapped the envelope on the corner of his desk.

"My meeting with MADD is by the post office. Want me to take that?"

Cheryl watched him for a few seconds. Maybe he was finally coming around. "Sure. Why not? Mail this delivery confirmation. I don't think they received the last one."

"I need to get back on this call. Will you pull the door, please?"

Cheryl regarded her husband, feeling the sting of his dismissal. They would talk today. Justin needed an attitude adjustment.

She was standing in the foyer, not knowing what to do now, when Chad cleared his throat. "Please, put me on Justin's schedule."

"No time today. The ambassador has a meeting with the chancellor at nine-thirty, followed by lunch with Congresswoman Mannette. The academic awards ceremony with the fifth-grade class at Sacred Hearts School is at three, photographs with the local MADD group at four, a strategy dinner meeting with staff, then a meeting at nine tonight. But if you'd like to have lunch, my schedule will always be free for you."

Frustrated, Cheryl squeezed her hands. She couldn't deny that there was something charming about the man four years her junior. He was handsome, intelligent, and interested in her. But she was married and he worked for her husband.

And she wouldn't ever cheat.

But Chad made her feel good. Maybe that's why she hadn't been more firm in her opposition. He made her feel like Justin used to.

"Chad, there could never be anything between us."

"Never is a long time. A lot can happen, especially when one party is feeling, and rightfully so, unappreciated."

His voice took on a gentle tone as he slowly moved closer to her. "Your husband may be blind to your unhappiness, but I'm not. I'll bet all you think about is him."

"That's right."

Chad touched a ringlet of hair that had escaped the ponytail. "But are you all he thinks about? If you were mine, I'd be concerned about being a good husband to my beautiful, sexy wife."

Justin's office door opened.

Chad didn't move although the door was right behind him. Nor did he acknowledge that Justin was now in the room.

His eyes remained fixed on her. "I'm sorry, Mrs. Crawford. The ambassador's schedule is packed solid. He won't be able to squeeze you in. You'll fly out of Ecuador tomorrow and arrive at ten in the morning. I've arranged for a car to pick you up from the airport, and I put a copy of your itinerary on your desk."

Cheryl wanted to run as if she'd been caught stealing from the candy jar. But Chad had changed the flow of their conversation without missing a beat.

As Justin regarded her, she almost couldn't speak. "You're not going to the funeral?" she asked him.

"Yes. I have a flight out at ten tonight."

"Why are we traveling separately?"

"I have a lot to do before we leave. I thought you might want to get a good night's rest. There's no reason for you to go early, anyway. I'm a pall-bearer."

Cheryl had stepped beside Chad, who blinked in a slow, bored manner before walking off. Chad's office door closed and she took in her husband's unapproachable stance. "Honey, I want to travel back to Atlanta with you."

"Cheryl, I need to get some work done." He looked distracted.

Now he was too busy to share a silent airplane ride to Atlanta with her? Why didn't he just tell her to stay here and not bother to come at all?

The dusting of esteem from Chad's attention drifted away under the aloof glare from Justin's eyes.

"What's happened to you?" Cheryl demanded. "You used to love for me to accompany you on trips."

"Things have changed. These matters are confidential."

"Okay," she said, still not understanding. She approached him and reached for his hand. "I promise not to disturb you, and if by some weird chance I hear something, I won't tell."

He squeezed her hand in a dismissive manner and went to the silver service on the sideboard. "Coffee?"

"No. Justin, what's going on?"

"I can't say," he said, not bothering to pour himself a cup.

"Not even to me? I'm getting scared."

He pressed his lips to her forehead. When she turned her mouth to receive his affection, he moved away.

"There's nothing for you to be afraid of. The staff is here and you'll be more than fine tomorrow."

"Justin, I'm traveling with you tonight."

"Cheryl—"

"Why can't I come with you?" she said so no one could overhear them. "I'm your wife. Are we safe? Should I call Jett?"

He hurried over. "I'm sorry, sweetheart. If it'll make you feel better, we can travel together," he said, abruptly changing his tune.

Relieved, she moved toward him. "Why haven't you responded to my note?" she asked softly. "You promised we'd deal with it, and so far, nothing."

He looked into her eyes. "I thought we'd dealt with it. You looked satisfied last night."

"Justin, did you even read what I wrote? I'm tired of this life. I'm tired of politics. You promised that after Jett went to college, I'd have my turn."

"I can't believe you were serious."

Incredulous, she gaped at him. "I'm never *not* serious. Well?" she demanded.

"We have to talk," he said, again moving away from her toward his office door.

"I thought we were talking."

"Cheryl, I don't have time for this discussion right now. I have to prepare a few words for the funeral, and before that, get through the rest of today. I've got to see Lea and Sam. Tomorrow's schedule has been crunched because of the funeral, and then I've got one of the most important meetings of my career."

"What meeting?" She threw up her hands. "Right, it's confidential. There used to be a time when we didn't have secrets. Now our lives revolve around your confidential encounters with God only knows who. I want you to quit, Justin. Resign and start living the life we promised to each other," she said in a level voice. "Otherwise, I don't know what's going to happen to us."

"That's ridiculous. Our life is great." He opened the door to his office. "Maybe you need a short vacation. Perhaps another trip to Puerto Rico. I never did find out the real reason you went there. By the way, Solomon Grossman expressed his thanks to you for visiting Eleanor."

So he knew. Cheryl refused to deny it. But why didn't he just come right out and ask her instead of justifying keeping his secrets because of hers?

"I'll be glad to talk to you about my trip."

"You don't have to," Justin said. "That's why we work, Cheryl. We respect each other."

He took in her dress and bare legs, and for the

briefest second she thought he was going to finally comment on her weight loss.

"It's supposed to rain. You might want to take an umbrella on your walk."

Justin's office door closed, shutting Cheryl out.

She hurried into the gardens and felt as if she were in another dimension.

Was her marriage over?

How could Justin so blindly disregard her feelings? They'd been together nearly twenty years and he'd promised she'd have her career after he made his mark in politics. Mentally she ticked off his jobs. Including being an attorney, he'd held ten in which he served his city, state, or country. From small-town city councilman to ambassador of Ecuador.

Why wasn't that enough?

Cheryl pulled a brochure of the university from her pocket and gazed at her dream. Five young women with graduation scrolls in their hands held them high as symbols of success. Cheryl's heart swelled with pride.

As an associate instructor of women's studies at the University of South Africa, she'd have the chance to shape the lives of women, just like those depicted in the photograph.

This job was the answer to her prayers. So why wasn't she ecstatic? Because she knew that Justin wouldn't be thrilled.

Meeting with the university recruiters in Puerto Rico last week had opened her eyes to the importance of the position that she was considering. She'd learned so much that the first night she'd been overwhelmed. As she'd lain in bed, she wanted to call Justin and share her thoughts with him, but she couldn't. He hadn't known she was there. And he wouldn't have approved.

She scuffed her sandal lightly on the cement. She'd never disapproved of anything he'd ever done. But somehow she'd known, even before their conversation today, that he wouldn't agree to leaving his job.

The wind whipped the brochure from her hand, dropping it outside Justin's office window. Cheryl carefully disentangled it from the bushes and stepped out of view.

Justin stood before Chad, Herb, and Maura, their eyes mesmerized by whatever he was saying.

A hundred years ago, she'd been that way with Justin. His very first cheerleader, secretary, office clerk, manager, and then his wife. She'd been proud of that honor.

But now that she wanted him to reciprocate the love and support she'd given him, she didn't know if he could.

Reality swept her. She'd always been looking in the window of their lives, waiting for the day when Justin would relinquish the spotlight and let her have her moment.

The paper flapped between her fingertips, the wind eager to take it away.

Cheryl backed away from the window and walked to her room. She passed their bed, and despite their fight her body stirred, reminding her of the times when nothing else but satisfaction mattered.

She'd become a sexual object for Justin to conquer each night. Had their coupling become his ultimate win?

Deep in the valley of her heart, Cheryl didn't believe that to be true.

For them, making love had never been just about sex.

In bed, intimacy bound them. The feel of his day-old beard as it scratched her neck and chin would flutter her heart because that meant he was inches from her mouth, facing her.

He could hear her.

As they lay entwined, she'd look into his eyes and they would communicate without words. And when she would speak, he'd say yes again and again.

Cheryl absently straightened the eyelet coverlet and walked to her closet where she began to pack.

She was laying out two business suits when her private phone rang. "Hello?" she said, stepping over to the wall of drawers and sliding one open.

"How'd things go?" Keisha asked.

With Keisha, Cheryl couldn't hide her disappointment. "Not great. I think he wants to serve the people forever."

Keisha had been Cheryl's sister-in-law for nearly twenty years. They agreed that when a woman had been selected by a Crawford man, she was his for life. And they loved their men, completely.

Although they had other wonderful sisters-in-law, they shared a special bond only time could create.

Keisha knew about the recruitment meeting,

but for a second Cheryl wished she hadn't shared so much. Now Keisha held her accountable for realizing her dream. "Did Justin say he wouldn't quit?" Keisha asked.

"Essentially."

"Truthfully, I didn't think he would."

"Thanks for sharing that now."

Keisha sighed in sympathy. "Honey, we both knew that'd be a hard sell. He's young and if Pops is any indication, Justin will be working for another forty-five years."

Cheryl lost her breath for a moment. Of course Keisha was right. But on the opposite end of the spectrum, that meant she was . . .

"I can tell by what you're not saying that you think you can't teach out of the country, because then Justin wouldn't be able to do his thing. I'm here to tell you that both are possible."

Cheryl swallowed the hard knot in her throat. "I don't appreciate that you know me so well."

Keisha laughed loudly and Cheryl couldn't help but chuckle.

"Why is this so hard? Why can't I just do what I want and have my husband support me?"

"Because a long time ago you gave him permission to achieve his dream and you promised that you'd always be by his side. Now you want some of that back, and he has to learn how to share. Not an easy thing for a grown man after having the whole pie to himself forever."

"He's not a child," Cheryl said of the man who'd just told her he was too busy playing God to grant her one request. "But he needs to know the world doesn't belong just to him."

"Good for you. Now . . ." Keisha's voice lowered. "What are you prepared to give up to get what you want?"

"What are you talking about? Give up? Nothing."

"Then he wins."

Frustrated, Cheryl snapped the suitcase closed. "We can both win."

"Not if his head is buried—"

"Keisha! Shut your nasty mouth." Cheryl's face heated up.

As the oldest sister-in-law of six, Keisha had a lock on being able to say anything.

Jade, Nick's wife, was a close second.

Although Cheryl had the years, she'd given up talking dirty and drinking with the girls. Because back in the day, if she had the right amount of the wrong things, she had been known to be wild.

"Now, see?" Keisha said. "I was going to say in the clouds, but call it what you like, if he can get his way he will. Since you brought it up, you might have to put up the sign 'closed until further notice.'"

The thought of not having sex with Justin made her feel weak. Cheryl sat at her secretary, the phone pressed to her ear. "I don't know," she said, feeling more doubtful than she sounded. "I *like* it."

Keisha's guttural laugh petered off. "I know. Crawford men can work magic in the bedroom, but in your case, that's the only place you're getting any satisfaction, right?"

What could Cheryl say? She was right. "Yes."

"So then you have to give him some incentive to change. Hey," Keisha said to someone else. "Hold on, Cheryl."

No sex? For how long? That was all they had at the moment.

The telling confession didn't pass her lips, but filled her heart with sadness. If she didn't stop the cycle, her husband would make love to her until she died. With her completely and utterly unhappy.

"Hey," Keisha said in a hurry. "I've got to run."

"Everything okay?"

"Yeah, but—"

"Tell me when I get home," Cheryl said, not wanting to hold her up. "We're coming in tonight. I'll call you when we arrive."

"Good. Love you," Keisha said and hung up in Cheryl's ear.

"Bye." Cheryl docked the phone slowly and went back into her closet to change.

She stopped back at her desk, called the airport, and changed her flight. Then she consulted her PDA and dialed from her cell phone. "Mr. Hill, This is Cheryl Crawford," she said to the recruiter. "Please set up the meeting with me and President Mandeke." She listened for a moment. "I understand the process could take some time. If you have additional questions, please don't hesitate to call me on my cell phone. I'll be in Atlanta for the remainder of this week. Thank you."

Cheryl hung up, gathered her purse and suitcase, and was out the door before she remembered one important item. She slipped into the room and emerged, the brochure tucked safely in her bag.

Teaching had always been her dream, and if this opportunity in South Africa worked out, her dream would become a reality. With or without Justin.

Five

The navy blue suit, white blouse, and a strand of Chinese pearls made Cheryl feel comfortable, although the interview with the president of the University of Johannesburg and the chancellor of student affairs didn't.

They'd gotten off on the right foot talking about the goals of the curriculum she'd selected, but had veered astray when the chancellor had criticized African-American women. He suggested that they could take lessons from their African sisters when it came to work ethics.

Cheryl regarded Mr. Auboudke. "Sir, why did you ask me to join you in expanding the minds of your female students?"

The president interrupted. "Please excuse my learned colleague. He is skeptical about an American teaching the women's studies class because of the very free and open society you live in. You only have to watch television videos to understand his concern."

"Dr. Mandeke, you are the president of a college." Cheryl smiled at him. "Surely you are not judged by the actions of every one of your students."

He scoffed. "That is correct."

"Then is it fair to judge me by the actions of a few teenagers?"

"Mrs. Crawford," Chancellor Auboudke interrupted. "Our young women see the imported magazines, and they want to have the lives of the women on the pages. How will you tell them that is not possible?"

Cheryl folded her hands. "Why can't they have any life they choose?"

"It is unrealistic. Our women need to raise our families."

"Sir, societal issues notwithstanding, that is the purpose of a university. To teach students how to expand their minds so that they can enrich the lives of the people around them. Now, I'm not holding this class up to be a life-altering experience, but I think the women who take the course deserve to know about women from many cultures, including the ones they see on TV and in magazines."

When neither said anything, she changed the subject. "I understand the university provides housing for visiting faculty? Is it near the university?"

"Yes," the president said, his chest inflating. "We were the first institution to offer such a perk for our staff. The rent is reasonable too."

"Probably nothing you're accustomed to," the chancellor said, his mouth twisted.

"Thank you for your concern, but I'm sure it's more than adequate. I appreciate the university's generosity."

As Cheryl studied the two men, she was glad

she'd dressed conservatively because her curriculum would be controversial.

In addition to magazines, she'd include course material on women from India, England, Italy, and other African countries. The big surprise was that she'd have guest speakers from all over the world, and that would cause a stir.

Cheryl had no intention of being quiet or politically correct. This course was about women, for women. Cheryl bet that before the first week was over, she and Chancellor Auboudke would be at it again, because his mentality was one she'd be fighting first.

A heated exchange erupted between the two men and ended abruptly.

"President Mandeke has indicated that he feels my comments may be deemed argumentative. I don't mean to offend you," the chancellor said.

"I'm coming into your country to teach your students. I understand there will be concerns. I hope to resolve some now, if possible."

"That's good to know, Mrs. Crawford, because while a small population of people will welcome you, you will be resented for supporting ideas that will undoubtedly take young women from our country. Our people are our resources. We can't afford to lose the healthy ones."

The honest revelation stopped Cheryl's thoughts that the man was a bigoted jerk. "I appreciate your honesty. South African women are no different than those from other countries. They have minds of their own. Stifling them will only bring about resistance. Educating them will hopefully bring about understanding."

The president slid a letter across the table and Cheryl read it from beginning to end. The salary was adequate, but not what the recruiter had mentioned.

"I trust this is comparable to my male colleagues?"

The two men looked markedly uncomfortable. "Why, yes. With a slight adjustment for the housing benefit."

Cheryl wrote down a figure before sliding it across the table.

The president looked at the amount, then cast a startled glance at her.

"You can get someone cheaper, but not better. And I'll bring my own supplies."

"This is acceptable," he said, and folded the letter into his breast pocket. "Will you be traveling with your husband?"

Just the thought of Justin brought about dual feelings of guilt and apprehension. "Why do you ask?"

"If the ambassador accompanies you, we can offer accommodations in the same units as other faculty and their families. If the ambassador won't be accompanying you, you would then be placed in the unmarried faculty housing and given an escort."

"Why is that necessary?"

"For your safety. You will be a single woman traveling daily to and from an environment you are not yet accustomed to. Mrs. Crawford, we would do this for anyone."

Cheryl considered their offer. There was no reason to be difficult. As long as the rules applied to everyone. "My husband will be accompanying me to Africa."

The men looked up in surprise. The chancellor even seemed to have more respect in his gaze. "What an unexpected pleasure. Perhaps we can put him to work too."

Cheryl gave them a noncommittal smile. "Perhaps."

The president leaned forward. "We discussed your start date of June sixth. Is that a problem? I know you have several households and other business matters that have to be dealt with before your two-year commitment to us begins."

Cheryl appreciated his gentle inquiry. She could tell she would enjoy President Mandeke. "Two months is more than enough time for me to conclude my business in the States."

"Excellent. If you are in agreement, we will proceed with the final stages of the hiring process and we'll have a final letter to you within the week. Well, I promised to keep you only an hour and we've exceeded that time. It is an honor to meet with you again, Mrs. Crawford. Please don't hesitate to contact me if you have additional questions or concerns."

"Good day, gentlemen." Cheryl left the building exhilarated. This was the beginning she had sought. Now she had to break the news to her husband that they were leaving.

Six

The early evening meeting had been pulled together at the last minute and Justin was feeling the ravages of a long day.

He sat across from Tommy Ahern and five Atlanta businessmen who had shared their ideas for the state of Georgia, and wondered how much more they needed from him. He was anxious to see Cheryl. Her stunt yesterday of leaving him in Ecuador had affected his ability to concentrate all day.

He leaned into the conversation and focused. The men had discussed his "winability factor," a term he'd never heard before, and how best to get his name before the voting public.

These six men were collectively worth more than seventy billion dollars, but their influence had greater value. Their support would weigh heavily with older voters, as well as employees of the conglomerates they controlled.

Justin believed that if he won over this group, he'd be ready for anything the voters threw his way.

For the past two hours they'd quizzed him about his position on everything from education to unemployment, attracting businesses to Georgia, the state of the country, and politics under the current administration.

Justin hadn't talked about himself or his views at length for a long time. He was exhausted, but it was a good exhaustion. The meeting would be over within the hour, and he hoped that they'd have the kind of faith in him that he needed, if he decided to accept the senatorial nomination.

"If you're chosen, will you have the full support of your family?"

"I always have and always will."

"So your wife isn't considering other career avenues?"

"No," Justin said. As soon as the word left his mouth, he wished he could call it back. Cheryl did have career aspirations, only Justin couldn't imagine why. He gave her everything.

What had started as a tiny thread of guilt turned into a skein. He'd found Cheryl's letter, read it, and put it away for safekeeping. Surely she could understand that his work as a senator would help far more people than a handful of students taking a class at a college in Africa.

Bubba Franklin had asked the question about Cheryl's career aspirations and now furrowed his brow as if he knew something Justin didn't. As COO of the airport in Atlanta, Franklin was sharp. "What about the grant you're trying to procure for the country of Ecuador? If this opportunity comes through first, you'll have to resign your position and get back to Georgia to campaign."

Justin's guilt multiplied. "I believe in the work

I've done there. It would be small-minded of me to think that I am the only man that could see that project to fruition. The country deserves that grant. And if I'm asked to run, I'll make sure the right people are in place for the process to continue without me."

Several of the men nodded.

Tommy spoke up. "If we had an endorsement from Lea North, that would make the transition easier. Mr. Crawford, how do you feel about asking for her support?"

"I don't have a problem with it."

"Any nasty skeletons in your closet? We've been surprised before," the COO of the largest phone system in the Southeast said.

"My life is clean, and I'm proud of it."

"Then you won't have a problem with an extensive background check?"

"None. I have nothing to hide."

"I think we've done enough for one day," Joseph Washburn, the president of a major soft drink conglomerate, said, and gave Justin a supportive thumbs-up. "Let's meet at week's end. Before then I'm sure members of your political party will want your attention. Your name has been bounced around in many influential circles."

"I'm pleased to hear that."

"Crawford, these talks are confidential," Washburn continued. "Hopefully not for long."

Justin understood that the rest of the process would take place behind closed doors. Before anything could be made public, he'd have to meet with his accountants to procure money for the campaign.

The gentlemen rose and extended their hands, signaling the end of the meeting. "Thank you, Ambassador. We'll be in contact."

"I appreciate your time," Justin said, the wheels turning as to who would be the best campaign strategist, manager, and spokesperson.

Tommy walked him to the door. "Keep your head down, but get prepared," he said. "We're a step closer. You'll hear from me soon."

Justin got into his car and headed to the courthouse, where he knew his father would be, but then changed his mind and headed to his parents' house.

Several of his brothers had been at the funeral, and would probably be at the house since he and Cheryl were home.

Right now he needed to see his wife. Her brief appearance at the funeral had filled him with embarrassed guilt. Nobody left a funeral reception without saying something to the bereaved, but that was exactly what Cheryl had done.

All he remembered was the black, wide-brimmed hat that had accentuated her sculpted neck.

Justin shifted in his seat, his body stirring at the memory. Cheryl had always been a full-bodied woman, but today she'd looked, well, voluptuous.

He'd missed making love to her last night, and now she was on his mind. He wondered if she missed him. Obviously not. She'd made a scene about him planning to come to Atlanta without her. Then she'd left him!

What had gotten into her?

He pushed aside the niggling of guilt that had pricked him on the flight from Ecuador to Atlanta. He'd sacrificed his life to work for his country, and now one private dream was on the brink of becoming reality.

Justin could only see one answer.

He wouldn't allow anyone to stand in the way of him becoming the next senator for the state of Georgia.

Seven

Light as air, Cheryl was tripping down the steps of Georgia State University, soaking up the warm sunshine, when a bouquet of fresh flowers was thrust into her path.

She followed the arm up. "Chad, what are you doing here?"

"Congratulating you, I hope."

"How did you know?"

He unfolded a copy of the letter she'd asked Justin to mail for her weeks ago in Ecuador. "Where'd you get this?"

"Do we really need to go there, or can I convince you to let me buy you a celebratory cup of coffee?"

"Oh." She hesitated.

She was pretty sure that Justin would be looking for her by now. But then again . . . he had never looked for her. She'd always been right there.

"Come on, Cheryl. I'm not asking you to sleep with me. It's coffee and I'm thirsty." He wiggled his arm. "I brought you flowers."

Why not? She'd been home for two days and

Justin hadn't paid her a bit of attention. She accepted the bouquet.

"Okay, one cup and then I have to skedaddle."

Chad eyed her. "What did you just say?"

Unsuccessfully she tried to hide her smile and started walking. "Nothing."

"Is that some form of walking? I don't think I've seen that before. Demonstrate," he demanded, a few steps behind her. A low whistle brought her around. "If that's it, skedaddling is my new favorite pastime."

"Chad," she warned, gesturing with the flowers. "We both know the deal."

"That we do," he said, guiding her to his rental car. "Doesn't mean I don't wish the cards were being dealt in my favor. How was the interview?"

He changed the subject so fast, Cheryl felt foolish referring to things he'd said two comments ago. "The interview went well. There's one professor, a chancellor actually, who doesn't want me there. He thinks I'm going to turn the women away from the men."

"Is that your plan?"

"Of course not," she defended. "They invited me to teach women's studies. We won't be just covering American women. In fact, Western women was going to be last on the syllabus. Why aren't you in Ecuador?"

"I thought life would be more interesting here." He tooled the Navigator out of the lot and headed toward Midtown. They passed a Starbucks on Peachtree, and Cheryl made a mental note to stock up on coffee before she moved. Atlanta's traffic she could live without, but Starbucks coffee she couldn't.

Chad drove past another Starbucks and she pointed. "That's the second one you've passed. Where are we going?"

"Phipps Plaza. I figured we could get something to drink while I have the jeweler take a link out of my watch. It's too big." He showed her.

Cheryl sat quietly. She loved shopping at Phipps Plaza. Their boutique stores carried unique items. And Nordstrom's was to die for. But the diehard elite still shopped at Phipps, and if she was seen . . . Justin might get the wrong impression.

Good, she decided. Maybe then he'd realize her worth. Besides, nothing improper was going on.

"If you're concerned about your image, I can carry your bags and address you as Mrs. Crawford."

In all her thirty-eight years, Cheryl had never been more embarrassed. Chad was very much a man, and not her servant.

"I would never ask or expect that from you, Chad. I have an image to protect. I will not embarrass my husband. I'm sure you understand. You've been in politics long enough to know the deal."

"If it looks like a fish, make it stink like one," he said, quoting the publicists' motto.

They pulled into the covered parking lot and trolled the lanes slowly, looking for a space.

Cheryl peered out the window. "You do understand. I'm glad we're friends, Chad."

Jaw set, Chad didn't speak.

A red Cabriolet darted out and Chad slammed on the brakes, throwing out his arm to stop her forward trajectory.

Cheryl grabbed the seat and held on as the three blond passengers and their "just back from spring break" driver realized her error and laughed before pulling away.

"Did I ever mention I don't think Georgia should be a right-to-procreate state?" he asked, as he took advantage of the vacant space.

Heart racing, Cheryl laughed and let her body relax.

"You want little Chads or Chadettes, don't you?"

They got out of the truck, and Chad came around to walk beside her.

"If my kid's name is Chadette, definitely not. It's the act of almost having a baby I'm most interested in."

Bold and in charge, Chad led the way to the door of the mall and held it open for her.

They headed to Starbucks and Cheryl ordered her favorite latte grande. Chad placed his order and paid, then headed out into the mall where they strolled.

"How does the ambassador feel about you teaching?"

"He supports me." Cheryl told the lie, then stopped. "I haven't mentioned it since we left Ecuador."

"That's the way to go. Think he might miss

you not being here while you're in Africa? That continent isn't around the corner."

"Can we change the subject? I was enjoying my high from the interview."

He glanced at her and smiled. "I'm glad you took me up on my offer for coffee. When were you going to tell me?"

"I wasn't, to be quite honest. We're not like that, Chad. I feel honor-bound to talk to my husband and family first."

"So where do I fit in?" he asked, rounding a corner that had been vacated by the Sak's Fifth Avenue store. This end of the mall received little traffic, so they were virtually alone.

"Why isn't my friendship enough?"

"Because I see a woman who isn't happy, whom I find incredibly attractive. I feel that all that's standing in the way of us finding out if there could be anything between us is her husband—a man who treats her like she's invisible."

Cheryl's throat closed, and unexpected tears sprang to her eyes. She turned around blindly, until her emotions were under control.

Why did his truth hurt so much? Even knowing that Chad was attracted to her pierced her insides, marring the picture she'd framed of her life that up until now had been unremarkable.

She'd been Justin's wife since her late teens, and soon she'd be pushing her next major birthday. Now that she knew what she wanted to do with her life, she saw that her husband's dream could stand in the way of her future.

Cheryl wasn't sure what to do.

Chad handed her an expensive handkerchief,

but Cheryl shook her head. "I'm fine, thanks. I don't know what to say, Chad. I've never led you on. You've always known your position, and mine—I didn't mean that the way it sounded. I'd like for us to be friends."

He backed her into a large pole and pressed his body against hers.

"Let's get something straight. I get a hard-on every time you and I are within the same city block. I'm not your damned friend. I'm the man who's trying to take you from your husband."

"Chad—"

Before she could complete her sentence, his mouth claimed hers. Tiny rockets went off inside her head. *What's happening? Can anyone see us?*

Cheryl's hands came up between them and he slowly backed off. "I'm not sorry for our kiss. You're not invisible to me, Cheryl. Remember that." He touched her jaw with his thumb. "I don't want you to regret any of this. Shall I take you back to your car?"

The coffee container frozen to her hand, Cheryl remained still, her lips tingling, her brain buzzing. "No, please go. I'll get a taxi."

She waited a few minutes, trying to get her bearings. Maybe no one saw them. Maybe she'd get away with this minor level of infidelity without pictorial documentation.

Cheryl dropped the coffee into the trash, turned in the opposite direction, and ran straight into her son, Jett, and his girlfriend, Kathy.

"What the hell is going on?"

"Son, it's not what you think."

"I'll give you two some privacy," Kathy said, and

before Jett could protest, she guided her wheel-chair into an exclusive store.

With Kathy gone, Cheryl faced her son's confused and hurt expression. "It looked like Chad was kissing you, Mom."

"He was, I mean he did, but we're not having an affair. We're not having anything."

"Then what was that all about?"

"He likes me, and he's been a good friend. But I made it clear that I love Justin and that I'd always be true to my marriage. That's all, darlin'. I promise."

"Mom, you're not a liar and I don't think you'd go around cheating on Dad. I trust you, but if he feels like that, you need to stay away from him. Even the best person in the world can be tempted."

"I know, Jett." She didn't elaborate for fear she'd dig herself into a deeper hole. She should have seen it coming and she hadn't. Cheryl wasn't at all pleased with her behavior for letting things get that far out of control.

"Where are you two heading?"

"We were just picking up a few things. Want to come with us?"

"Sure. I wanted to get a present for the baby." As they walked, Cheryl glanced around, discreetly. She and Chad couldn't ever do that again. If anyone had seen them, besides her son, they could have wound up in major trouble.

Eight

The blocks rolled by as Justin neared his parents' home.

He checked in with Maura, then hung up, knowing he'd have to make a decision as to the employment of his staff.

They might not want to work for him now that he'd chosen to pursue the Senate seat. They'd have to relocate—again. And Maura had found someone in Ecuador. Justin didn't know anything about the guy, except that there was one. Chad had told him.

Justin turned onto the block his parents had lived on for twenty years. His memory faded back to the day he and Cheryl married. She'd been so happy. Nothing like the woman she was now, with her sad eyes. The light that used to burn eternal in the brown depths had all but died.

He blinked the image from his mind. Cheryl would come around. He was running for the United States Senate to help better America. Once she understood the need for his leadership, she wouldn't be able to say no.

Justin parked down the street and walked toward the house, using the time to think.

Cheryl said she wanted to teach, but he wasn't sure she was aware of the challenges. Africa was the mother continent, but many of the citizens struggled in ways that Americans had no knowledge of.

His wife was an excellent hostess, fluent in three languages, and could become an expert at anything she put her mind to. Truly, he wouldn't be where he was without her. As far as he was concerned, their goals *were* the same.

Except . . . she wanted him to quit his job.

The opportunity of a lifetime lay at his feet and Cheryl wanted him to walk away. Justin just couldn't fathom his life without his work, and the stirrings of anger began. For nearly twenty years, he'd made a life for them as a public servant. Why should he quit just because Cheryl wanted him to? That wasn't fair to him or to his constituents.

Maybe Jett could talk to his mother, but Justin nixed the idea. Father and son agreed on one thing, that they couldn't agree on anything. Justin was heading around to the back of the house and approached the screened porch when he heard the women in the breakfast room.

"Cheryl, you look hot! How much weight have you lost?"

The voice sounded like his sister-in-law Jade, but she was supposed to be in the hospital, having her baby. Damn! He'd forgotten to tell Cheryl. Now they wouldn't have a present.

But that couldn't be Nick's wife. Not even kickass Jade would be so tough as to leave the hospital within a few hours of having a baby.

Justin waited for his wife's reply.

"Thirty pounds and counting."

Damn, he thought. That was significant.

"I wish I could lose thirty pounds."

That *was* Jade.

"If you'd stayed at the hospital, you would have lost it by now by having that baby," Keisha chimed in. "But Ms. 'I've got a gun' thinks she can control everything, including when her baby is born."

The other sisters-in-law laughed.

"Enjoy it while it lasts because this is the very last thing you'll control when it comes to a Crawford," Lauren, his brother Eric's wife, added. She'd only been in the family seven years, but she knew the truth.

"What does Justin think of your sexy new shape?" Terra, Michael's wife, asked.

"He hasn't said," Cheryl replied.

"What?" several chorused. "Is he blind?"

"I don't know."

Silence hung for a moment before the sound of aluminum foil tearing and being wrapped on bowls filled the air.

"I'm sure he's very busy," Terra offered, always the peacekeeper.

"He'd miss a leg, and that weighs about thirty pounds," Keisha added. "You should tell him about himself."

Justin wondered how he could miss the fact that his wife had lost so much weight. His attention had been devoted to securing the grant for Ecuador.

He missed her. He'd make it up to her tonight.

"Where is Justin?" Jade asked, sounding strained.

"He was at the funeral." Cheryl sounded indifferent, as if his movements didn't matter one way or another.

"But where is he now?" Keisha pressed.

"I don't know. I left the Norths' home before him. I didn't want to disturb him and his friends."

Justin could feel the vein in his forehead bulging. Another secret? What the hell was she up to? And why did he sound so terrible when Cheryl spoke of him?

"What's wrong, Cheryl?" Lauren asked, concerned. "You don't look happy."

"The truth is that Justin and I—"

He strained to hear.

"Oooow. These contractions hurt."

"Breathe," Keisha told Jade, the RN in the family. "Out slowly. Honey, aren't you ready to go back to the hospital? Your contractions are five minutes apart."

"They've been holding at six all day. No, I'll go when they're three minutes apart. I've got time."

"You know what they say about hard heads," Keisha told her lovingly.

"I know. They have soft behinds. Lucky for me, my ass is made of cement." Jade struggled to catch her breath, but no one was dragging her through the door, so he guessed she was staying put until she got ready.

He should tell Nick his wife was having intense labor pains, but Nick and Jade had a sixth sense about each other. He'd know when she was ready to go.

Justin wondered when he'd stopped knowing his own wife so well.

A ball smacked him in the back and he jerked around and moved away from the window. "Hi works," he said to his brothers, Michael, Julian, Eric, and Nick. He tossed the basketball back and shrugged off his suit jacket as they headed toward the basketball court.

"That's how we treat Peeping Toms," Julian replied, tossing the ball to Nick.

"Then we beat the hell out of them," the USMC colonel responded. "Any reason why you're listening to your wife instead of talking to her?"

Justin loosened his tie with one hand and with the other smacked the ball away. He and Nick scrambled, but he came up with it and took the jump shot for two. It circled the rim and fell off.

"My wife and I are just fine, thank you. Jade's contractions are five minutes apart."

Nick didn't blink as he rebounded the ball and went up for a dunk. The rim shook, but the shot counted. "She's a trooper. She'll let me know when she's ready. This conversation wasn't about me," he said, barely out of breath the way the other brothers were. "Why is your wife so unhappy?"

Julian stripped the ball from Nick and shot from the right forward position for two.

"She's having a midlife crisis," Justin said.

Michael laughed as he dribbled to the top of the key, shot, and made it. "You're asking for a fight, aren't you? Midlife crisis? If you knew what was good for you, you'd expunge that from your vocabulary." He took the ball out and fed it to Nick.

"But he doesn't know what's good for him." Nick made a regretful noise before he knocked the ball down for another two points.

The scoreboard his family had installed tracked Justin's points at zero, while the others had scored.

Justin hustled for the rebound, but his shoes weren't flexible and he stumbled, while Nick came up with the ball.

"Fine," Justin said. "Cheat if it makes you feel better. I know what's good for me, and I know what's good for my family. We're going through growing pains. But otherwise, we're all right. Thanks for asking," he said, scrambling for the ball.

His brothers laughed and Justin could feel his competitive nature rising. He swiped at the ball Michael now held, but missed, then turned around. They had him in the center of a square, passing the ball over and around him.

Just what the hell did his brothers think they were doing? He didn't need to be schooled. His life was almost perfect.

Julian passed him the ball and for one second, relief ebbed through Justin's anxiety. Finally someone was on his side.

His ego deflated a second later when Nick stole the ball, fed it to Michael, who shot from the top of the key again and scored. Justin kept his anger at bay. This was psychological warfare.

Julian set a pick and leaned on Justin hard. "If Cheryl was all right, there wouldn't be a rental car in front of the house. If she was all right, she would have brought a present for Nick and Jade's baby, and if she was all right, the women would be on the porch watching us, instead of having a family meeting about us. Whatever you did, you'd better fix it."

Justin pushed his brother off and Julian stumbled. They went after each other and ended up face-to-face.

"Stay out of my business," Justin told him.

"Fix your family and I will."

"What do you know about my life, Julian?"

"Obviously more than you," Julian retorted. "Don't fuck around until it's too late."

Julian cursing at Justin was tantamount to a punch in the gut. "Don't tell me—"

The back door to the house smacked the wall. "Nicky," came Keisha's excited cry. "Come quick."

Every father on the court raced for the kitchen, Nick hurdling the porch in one leap.

By the time Justin reached the door, pandemonium had broken loose. Jade's contractions were two minutes apart.

His mother, Vivian, entered the kitchen and ushered Nick and Jade, Keisha and Eric, his brother whose specialty was delivering babies, into the lower bedroom and shut the door.

Terra, Michael's wife, rushed into her husband's arms, tears flowing. He took her onto the screened porch and held her as she talked.

Justin recalled something about them not being

able to have children, but he wasn't sure what was going on. Under different circumstances he would have checked on them, but after the basketball game he didn't want to take the chance of being told off.

He turned his attention to Julian, Lauren, and Cheryl, who had formed a prayer circle and were already too involved for him to join in. He felt excluded.

Quietly he went upstairs and retrieved towels and sheets and brought them back down.

The door to the bedroom opened momentarily and he caught a glimpse of the makeshift hospital room. Nick kneeled by the bed, his and Jade's hands clasped, his lips pressed to her forehead.

The door closed, but the image remained. He'd done the same thing when Cheryl was giving birth to their son nineteen years ago. A lifetime. They'd been so close. Had shared so much. Justin wasn't sure when the last time was that he'd kissed her—her letter had . . .

Just as he thought of Cheryl, she walked up to him. Maybe now they could talk. "Hi," he said.

"I'll take these inside." Her hands barely touched his, but the current that went through him tingled to the soles of his feet. He wanted to catch her hands, but he was still holding the fluffy cloth. Cheryl never looked up as she removed the linen from his hands, went into the room, and shut the door.

Justin waited outside the door for ten minutes, but felt silly when Cheryl didn't return.

Back in the kitchen, Lauren moved with ease

around the airy room, humming a tune he knew was her latest hit, a slow sexy song called "Loving You." "I like your new song," he said, at a loss for words. He hoped she wouldn't quiz him on the words, because he didn't know any. He just wanted someone to talk to.

She smiled and crinkled her pretty nose. "Was I humming that again? I try not to sing my songs too much for fear I'll tire of them." Her eyes danced as she kept wiping.

"Can I help?" he asked, feeling helpless.

"Keep positive thoughts," Lauren said, giving him a gentle smile. Seeing her here now, he never would have guessed that her single remix of "Silken Love" had bumped Beyoncé's new single from the number-one slot on Billboard. Coupled with her new single, Lauren's career was on fire.

Justin considered asking about her work, but didn't feel it appropriate at this moment.

She made two pitchers of iced tea, stirring mint leaves in one for his diabetic father. He grabbed the spoon and waited while she poured sugar into the other one.

"You sure you don't want to go out on the deck with Terra and Michael?"

The couple was sitting on one of the comfortable couches, her head resting on his shoulder.

"They look like they need some privacy. Where'd Julian go?" he asked as he stirred.

"To get cleaned up and check on the kids."

Justin took in his appearance. "Uh, I should . . ."

"Abandoning me already?" she asked, her mouth quirked.

Justin was grateful for Lauren's easy humor.

At least she didn't hate him. She took the spoon and gave his back an encouraging pat. "Go ahead. They may be a while."

Although he took his time, Justin was back in ten minutes.

Cheryl left the room for a few minutes and conferred only with Lauren, who then dialed 911. "This is Dr. Eric Crawford's wife, Lauren Crawford. Yes, it is me. No, this isn't a joke. We need an ambulance at 13436 Azalea Way Drive." She began to smile. "No, this isn't a life-threatening emergency. My sister-in-law is having a baby. Dr. Crawford is delivering it now. A backup on Twenty has both lanes closed."

"She's stabilized," Cheryl whispered to Lauren, who relayed the information.

"Could be an hour, or they can send a heli-copter."

Cheryl shook her head. "Eric said no."

She hurried back inside while Lauren wrapped up the conversation.

When Lauren hung up, it seemed as if the clock had started all over again.

They could hear Eric's gentle instructions, while Keisha assisted with monosyllabic answers to Eric. Nick encouraged his wife and Justin could hear faint praises from Cheryl.

The low murmuring sound was his mother, praying.

The back door smacked the wall and Justin's head wrenched up.

"What's going on?" his son Jett asked.

Justin was glad to see him. They hadn't been

together since Christmas. "Jade's having her baby," Justin told him.

"Here? She's crazy. I told her I'd drive her to the hospital, but she's a chicken."

Just as casual as high winds at noon, Jett blew into the house.

Justin wanted to tell him to quiet down, but Jett merely acknowledged his presence with a nod.

He kissed Terra, shook hands with Michael, and grabbed Lauren in a bear hug that made her giggle. "Put me down, crazy man."

Justin wasn't sure he was seeing things correctly. His son had spent the better part of his junior and senior years in Ecuador, yet after only one semester at Tech he'd obviously been around the family enough to become quite comfortable.

He walked up to the door of the impromptu delivery room and banged.

"Jett! Get away from there," Justin said, reaching for his arm.

Jett glared at him in defiance. "Jade? It's Jett. Hurry up and deliver my nephew so I can take him for a few beers down at Tech."

They all heard what sounded like a laugh. "I'll shoot you first, little boy."

Justin stepped back as Jett's face lit up. "I'm really scared. For real, though, you okay?"

"Wait . . . one . . . second."

After another strangled cry, they heard the sound of a tiny squall.

Everyone came into the kitchen, laughing and hugging. The baby kept crying and after ten minutes the door opened.

Jett was the first one inside. The new mom passed her baby to the big teenager she obviously had a good relationship with.

Justin watched in amazement as no one gave his son instructions on how to handle the infant. He just seemed to know.

"Jett, meet your niece, Jada Vivian Crawford."

He cradled her in his arms, his face as tender as when he'd been an innocent child himself. "You're a girl," he said, awed. "What a princess. Uncle Nick, you're going to need a very big gun. She's a hottie."

Everyone laughed as he placed the child in her mom's arms. He kissed Jade on her cheek. "She did good, didn't she?" he said to Jada's father, who held more love in his eyes than Justin had ever seen.

Nick's eyes glistened. "The best. How about we let the rest of the family get in here for a quick minute before Eric gives us our next instructions?"

Eric read Jade's blood pressure again and checked on his new niece. Lauren went to her husband's side and they talked privately. He kissed her lips, then turned into a doctor again.

"You have about five minutes. The ambulance will be here in short order to transport the new family to the hospital to be checked out."

Justin didn't realize he'd gravitated to Cheryl's side until it was their turn to congratulate the new family. Cheryl pulled a box from behind the chair Nick had settled into.

"I wasn't sure you had something for Jada to

come home in, so I thought you might like this, but, well, she's already home."

Nick kissed Cheryl's cheek and gave her a big hug. "Don't you worry. If she's anything like her mother, she'll need plenty of clothes."

Nick unwrapped the large box, and to Justin's amazement, pulled out a pretty pink and white one-piece jumper, with *I Love Mommy and Daddy* written in script across the front.

Jade's eyes teared as she looked between Justin and Cheryl. "How'd you know?" she asked. "*We* didn't know."

Cheryl shrugged. "Lucky guess."

"My mom is brilliant, right, Dad?"

Justin didn't miss the sarcasm in his son's voice. "She's pretty amazing."

They moved into the hallway and Justin reached for Cheryl's hand. She looked at how their palms met, as if him touching her was odd. Slowly her hand slipped from his. "Jett, I didn't know you were coming so quickly."

"I got your message that Jade was here and decided to stop by. I was going to head back to Kathy's, if you don't mind."

"I don't mind at all."

"Hello," Justin said to his wife and son, displeased that they were ignoring him. "Hi, Jett. Good to see you, and who is Kathy?"

His son's sardonic laugh grated on his nerves. "You haven't once responded to my e-mails. If you'd read them, you'd know who Kathy was. In fact, I haven't heard from you about anything, but I did thank Maura for calling and telling me that Sam's father had died."

Jett kissed his mother's cheek and grabbed a dinner roll from a basket Lauren had just removed from the oven.

"Mom, catch you later."

The back door smacked open and closed.

"What the hell is his problem?" Justin demanded.

Michael, Terra, and Lauren made a beeline for the wide, long hallway that led to the dining room that seated the entire family. The door made a resounding click when it closed.

Eric entered the kitchen from the other hallway, grabbed a glass of water, and left, closing the bedroom door behind him.

Justin and Cheryl were alone for the first time since yesterday afternoon in Ecuador.

"I don't know that Jett has a problem," Cheryl said, her arms crossed.

"He's disrespectful and rude. Didn't you answer his e-mail?"

"Yes, Justin, but he wasn't talking about me. He was talking about you."

"You, me, what's the difference? He heard from us. I thought that was the point."

"Then you missed his point entirely." Cheryl walked into the pantry and walked out with her arms laden with sweet potatoes.

Justin moved to help her, but Cheryl's look stopped him and she unloaded them onto the table.

Seeing her defined arms and sculpted legs stirred his body. Whatever was happening between them hadn't slackened his sex drive.

"You left me in Ecuador," he said.

"You found your way, didn't you?"

"Cheryl," he said, tired of sparring, "why don't you get whatever it is off your chest so we can move on?"

"You know what I want, and if you're not willing to do the right thing, I don't think we have anything to move on to."

That sounded too much like a threat. "What are you saying?" Justin rubbed his hands over his head. His wife was talking crazy, as was his son.

Unable to figure either of them out, he laughed. "This is a bad dream."

"I agree. For the first time in my adult life, I realized I haven't been living my dream, but yours. I won't do it any—"

"I've been asked to fill Dan North's position and run for the U.S. Senate."

The half-peeled potato slipped from Cheryl's hand and fell into the glass bowl. "The Senate?"

"Cheryl, I know it's crazy, but the night Dan died I was approached. I've been in meetings with some of the most powerful businessmen in the state. They want me." He laughed. "Can you believe it?"

She smiled, yet his heart felt torn to shreds. "Yes, I can. Right after he died?"

"It sounds bad, but they were very respectful. They even want me to ask Lea for an endorsement. Do you know what this could mean for our family? How important the Crawford name will become? This is big, Cheryl." He reached for her.

Justin hugged his wife, glad to have shared his burden. Now she'd understand what had kept him busy these last few days.

After a few seconds, Cheryl shrugged herself out of his embrace and put the bowl of potatoes in the commercial-size subzero refrigerator.

"It is big, Justin." Seconds passed as she washed the peeler, then her hands. She dried both on the dish towel.

"What are you doing? I thought you were making dinner for everyone."

She looked around the kitchen as if she didn't recognize it. "I was, but I don't think so."

The wail of the ambulance siren snaked into the stiff silence.

"Is that it? I get a 'way to go' and half a hug from my wife?"

The bedroom door opened and everyone set about moving furniture so that the EMTs would have a clear passage.

Angry with Cheryl and Jett, Justin turned to his family. "I know this is a big moment, but I have great news."

His brothers and sisters-in-law stilled.

"I've been asked to run for Dan North's U.S. Senate seat."

As expected, his family erupted into raucous congratulations. He accepted them graciously as he looked at his wife, who'd taken up the post at the back door. The ambulance drivers headed up the driveway, the gurney between them.

"Justin, do you feel senatorial?" Keisha asked.

Justin grinned. "Yes, as a matter of fact I do."

Lauren looked at Cheryl first, then at him. "Have you already accepted?"

"Yes, basically."

"What do you think, Cheryl?" he asked.

Never in their marriage had Justin intentionally put his wife on the spot, but her behavior was
so out of character he hoped to shock her.

Julian entered the kitchen, took in the invisible
tug-of-war, and moved toward Cheryl.

She opened the door for the paramedics and
let them pass. Eric led them into the bedroom as
the rest of his family watched the drama in the
kitchen.

The back door didn't smack closed, but eased
shut under her gentle hand. But there was nothing gentle about the glint in her eyes. "Quit, or
else . . ."

Nine

"Where'd that come from?" Keisha asked Cheryl. "For months I've been telling you to grow a backbone. Today you did!"

Upstairs in the living room of the suite of bedrooms designated for the Crawford grand-daughters, Cheryl held her arms over her stomach, her sisters-in-law in various states of emotion.

"We shouldn't have spoken that way in front of everyone. I'm sorry." Cheryl's voice quivered. She had finally spoken up for herself.

Terra had been tearful earlier, but now sat primly on one of the sectional sofas.

Lauren, Eric's wife, had taken on the role of protector, now that Jade was temporarily occupied. She'd herded the women upstairs to the granddaughters' suite, and had *locked* the door.

No one locked out the Crawfords. And then there was Keisha, wired and ready to do battle.

But even as Cheryl held her position as reluctant leader of this group, she wasn't sure how they could help.

She wanted her husband back. There was so much more they could do with their lives, and it didn't have to be in a fishbowl or at the beck and call of every influential person that came along. Justin had a hard time saying no—except to her.

From the window she watched as Mom and Pop Crawford talked to the neighbors now that the ambulance had driven away. Pop had come home in time to meet his new granddaughter, see the happy parents off, and watch the rest of his sons and their wives head in two separate directions.

Pop had worked half the day as a superior court judge, deciding the fate of others, yet when Ma Vivian gingerly plucked a flower from the plethora of bushes, he breathed in the scent of the flower and followed his wife.

Ma had had her career while Pop had his. Somehow they'd managed to raise a family at the same time. Pop easily took her hand, bringing it to his lips as they walked. The tender gesture broke Cheryl's heart. She and Justin had lost so much.

Cheryl wished she were at their house here in Atlanta, then she wouldn't have to walk back through this house and face the family.

Her ultimatum had already caused a divide as her sisters-in-law gazed at her with trust and support in their eyes. Even Terra seemed to be coming around.

Cheryl knew the men were somewhere together, either beating the hell out of Justin, or plotting on how to bring her "around."

Jade would be disappointed she'd missed all the action.

"Cheryl, what do you want us to do?" Lauren asked.

All the love in the room was stifling. She'd kept the problems in their marriage so secret that she felt strange being on the receiving end of such devotion and sympathy.

"I don't want you to do anything. I shouldn't have aired our dirty laundry."

"Don't retreat into a hole," Terra said quietly. "You have a wonderful husband. We all do, but if you want him you have to fight for him."

"Wow." Keisha echoed the expression on the others' faces.

"Did you see the way he looked at you?" Terra's voice rose an octave. "You got his attention. Remarkable."

Keisha's laughter brought Cheryl around. "He about swallowed his tongue. We all did, darlin'. Any person bold enough to tell a Crawford man 'quit, or else' has got a huge set of jugs."

"Stop laughing!"

Keisha sobered. "I'm sorry."

Cheryl started to apologize, but Lauren grabbed both women's hands and brought them to the couch. "Do you love Justin?"

Cheryl's gaze bounced between her sisters-in-law. "Yes, I do."

"Then fight for your family," Terra said. "We'll support whatever decision you make."

Cheryl gathered strength from Terra's quiet confidence. "I've been offered a teaching position at the University of South Africa."

A collective gasp tore through the room before she was embraced by loving arms.

Cheryl wanted to melt. This was the reaction

she wanted from her husband, but feared would never happen.

"Oh my," Lauren said, as the realization of Cheryl's decision settled in. "You are a trouble-maker, aren't you?" Her angelic faced blossomed. "I think I love you even more."

For the first time all day, Cheryl smiled. She dragged in a cleansing breath.

"Are you going to accept the position?" Terra asked.

The words rushed out. "I want to. Yes."

"Were you serious about Justin quitting?" Lauren asked.

"We made an agreement that when Jett went to college I'd be able to pursue any career I wanted. I don't want to be a politician's housewife anymore. I want to be a teacher. I am a teacher."

She felt as if she'd just confessed in front of a roomful of recovering housewives. "I don't mean to offend anyone."

"You haven't," Lauren said, the highest-paid housewife of them all. "But if I know Justin, he's going to do his best to sway you. When are you going to tell him about your job offer?"

"He knows. He just hasn't said anything to me about going."

"Then it's going to hit the fan soon." Keisha paced as she talked.

"We'll be moving in two months. I have to get shots and a visa to teach abroad, tons of paper-work. I have a lot to do."

"How long is the assignment?"

"Two years."

"A third of a senator's term in office."

"Sit Justin down tonight and talk to him. Explain how you've been feeling and tell him what it is that you want," Terra advised. "Remind him of your agreement and how important it is that he keep his word to you. If you two just talk, you should be able to clear up this misunderstanding in no time flat."

Cheryl reached over and grasped her hand. "Thank you, I will." She'd always taken for granted that because Terra was so quiet, that she didn't have anything of value to offer. Big mistake, she realized.

"Talk to him while you're in bed," Terra suggested in a shy voice. "Michael is much more attentive the less I have on."

Her cheeks flamed, but Cheryl understood.

"Definitely," Lauren agreed.

"You need to get street on his ass," Keisha said, her hands on her ample hips. "You're too nice— nothing like the woman you used to be."

"We all have to grow up." Cheryl didn't want to remember the old days. They were too far behind her.

"Obviously you forgot how to be the real you under that expensive perfume and those silk suits. He was just a guy before and he's just a guy now. Would you whup another woman's behind for trying to wreck your home?"

"Who knows what anyone would do for the right reasons?" Cheryl said.

"Yes or no?"

Cheryl felt herself getting angry. "Yes."

"Good." Keisha's voice softened. "Then you'll always know what you're fighting for. And no bed. I told you before. I'm sorry, Terra, but once he gets her on her back, it's over. In fact, cut him off completely. Then you'll get somewhere. And if down the road you need moral support, we'll boycott sex with you as a show of solidarity."

"What? Why us?" Lauren demanded, clearly not wanting to take their support that far.

"I don't know," Terra said, unsure. "I think I'm addicted."

Keisha rolled her eyes. "If we're going to support her, we're going all the way. Agreed?" she demanded.

Both Lauren and Terra sighed. "Agreed."

All gazes were on Cheryl.

She'd hoped they wouldn't agree to something so—personal. After all, her problems weren't theirs. Besides, she loved making love to Justin. In bed they connected. But she also knew sex alone wouldn't save their marriage.

"If it comes to that, then okay," Cheryl finally said.

"What about Jett?"

Cheryl understood why Lauren asked. At twenty-five, her daughter Shayla had been banished to Mississippi by her father to grow out of her childish habits, and had fallen in love in the process. Now Shayla and her fiancé split their time between the new practice in Mississippi and her father's practice here in Atlanta.

Lauren's daughter was six hours away. South Africa was considerably farther. "I want Jett to stay here at Tech. He's an excellent student, and he has a great future as an architect, if he stays focused. Besides, by the time I return, Jett will be ready to graduate. I've made up my mind. Jett is staying here."

"One thing at a time," Keisha said, pulling Cheryl from a battle that hadn't even started. "First Justin, then Jett."

"You're right. Ladies, I appreciate everything you've done for me."

They all hugged until a knock on the door broke them up.

"Cheryl?" Justin said. "May I speak to you?"

Her hands were still on Lauren's and Terra's backs, and she felt their hearts start to race. Hers galloped, too.

Cheryl separated from the group and smoothed out her Tiffany necklace. She took a breath and opened the door. "Yes?"

Justin saw her posse of support, then looked at Cheryl, his deep gray eyes clouded with concern.

Her breath caught in her throat. He was more handsome now than the day she'd met him. Cheryl resisted reaching out and caressing his face. She wasn't as tall as he, but her cheek fit beside his if he bent his knees just a little.

He did and she leaned in, just a little.

Behind her someone cleared their throat, and Cheryl took a step back.

An awkward silence filled the hallway.

"Are you ready to go home? I thought we might talk," he said softly.

"Yes, I'll get my purse."

Cheryl gathered her things and kissed her sisters-in-law good-bye, relieved now that she'd confided in them. "I'll see you tomorrow," she said, and moved toward Justin, who stood in the doorway.

She turned sideways, but their bodies still touched. The brief connection started a fire in her core and she kicked the toe of his Kenneth Coles, trying to slip by.

Justin reached out and caught her against him. "You all right?"

Cheryl wondered if he'd done it on purpose. She disentangled herself from his chest and arms. "Yes. Let's go."

She had to watch him. If she didn't know better, she'd think her husband was trying to seduce her.

Keisha, Lauren, and Terra watched the couple awkwardly make their way out of the house. Justin went toward his car and Cheryl to her rental, before he caught up to her and guided her to his vehicle.

Justin was attentive and manly. The consummate Crawford man in trouble.

"Ten dollars says she sleeps with him tonight," Keisha said, watching from the window.

Lauren and Terra seemed to be of one mind as they quickly grabbed their bags and headed out of the suite. "I feel a drought coming on. Eric?" Lauren called.

The door to the grandsons' suite of rooms opened. "Baby?"

"You ready?" she asked, already down the hall, sliding up on her toes to kiss him. They had the whole evening. Their six-year-old son, Damon, was in Mississippi with Shayla for the weekend.

Terra and Michael met in the hallway and kissed tenderly. "I'm ready," she breathed into his mouth.

His hands slid down her waist to her backside. "You are at that."

Keisha winked at Julian as he made his way past the couples to his wife. "What the hell went on in there?"

She looked at him, feeling a hunger for her only love that had never ceased. She backed into the room. "Just sex talk."

Julian followed her in and locked the door. "Were you the teacher or the pupil?"

Keisha grinned as her husband of two decades lifted her off her feet and onto the bed. "Pupil."

"Show me what you learned, hot stuff."

"Gladly."

Ten

"I'm sorry," Justin said, and closed his cell phone. "I won't take any more calls."

"For how long, Justin? As it is, you've been on the phone for an hour. An hour and fifteen minutes ago, you asked me what I wanted to eat."

"That's right. We could go to 1850."

Cheryl waved her hand. "No. I want to go home. Besides, we didn't call ahead, so we can't just walk in."

"I can."

Cheryl kept her gaze trained forward. "I don't want to go out in public so we can be inundated by people. I thought we were going to talk."

"You're right." He turned onto their block. "Let's order in. We haven't done that in a long time. Chinese?"

She gave him a small smile. "That sounds nice."

Justin silently congratulated himself on getting something right. Take-out Chinese food was her favorite.

He pulled into their three-car garage and let down the automatic door.

Justin waited on the steps leading into the house while Cheryl performed a visual inspection. She missed nothing, including the garden spade that had been left on the worktable instead of up on its allotted hook. He'd speak to Jett about taking better care of the tools.

"Come on, new Auntie. I know you want to get off your feet."

Her eyes met his and Justin wondered if putting his foot in his mouth was his new chosen talent.

This time when Cheryl passed him, she took extra care and made sure their bodies didn't touch. She was upset with him and he had to make it better. Tonight he'd make sure everything was about her pleasure, her comfort, and her needs.

Investing time in his wife was something he'd neglected, and he hadn't needed the tongue-lashing from his brothers to tell him so.

Cheryl laid her purse on the kitchen counter and poured ice water for them both.

Justin consulted his PDA and dialed the restaurant. He placed their order, then turned to Cheryl, unsure how to broach the subject.

"Cheryl, do you have any questions about the Senate?"

"No."

The abrupt answer aborted the speech he'd prepared. As she casually strolled to the kitchen table, Justin struggled to find the right words. "Then what can I say that will help you understand what an incredible opportunity this is?"

"You can say whatever you like—"

"Good. I'd be walking into a situation that could mean great things for the state of Georgia. I'd work with the commissioner of labor to entice companies to keep jobs in our state rather than outsourcing them. I'd try to revive the HOPE scholarship like we did in Ecuador and keep the resources we cultivate home where they belong."

Justin talked long after their food had been delivered and eaten. Cheryl had remained quiet the entire time, but he hoped she could see his vision. Just thinking about becoming a senator had kept him awake at night. The possibilities were endless. His term would be short, sixteen months, but he could get a lot done. And then he could either run again or aim higher. "What do you think?"

Cheryl began clearing the table, tossing the cartons into the trash. "How much does this mean to you?"

"Everything, Cheryl. Not just to me, you too. This is a tremendous op—I know I keep saying that, but it is."

"If it's that important, then you should follow your heart."

Why did that statement sound so final? Cheryl was being abnormally morbid. "We'd be home— here in Georgia. You'd be just a few hours from your family in Columbus."

"But you'd have to live in D.C."

"Sure, but we'd be closer to Jett living in the States. We could do more things together."

She turned at these words and studied him closely. "Like what?"

"Oh . . ." Justin stumbled. "Uh . . . what would you like to do?"

"No," she said graciously. "You first."

"Cheryl, this is silly." Justin slowed down. Getting frustrated wouldn't help anything. "We could entertain friends we haven't been able to see in a while. You love to cook, and everyone who samples your food says how delicious it is. We used to talk about starting a charity. We'd be an influential couple in this state, role models, Cheryl. We'd be together."

"And what would I do?"

"What do you mean? You could do anything you want."

"Anything?"

The casual cadence to Cheryl's voice didn't deceive Justin. Earlier she'd threatened him, and if he didn't calm her frustration he could conceivably spend more time thinking about her instead of the campaign.

He followed as she extinguished lights before heading up the stairs. "You do everything so well. Many of the wives are perfect hostesses, and you are too," he rushed to add. "You could mentor a young woman, or join the various charities that the spouses of senators support. If I were you, I'd join the spouses' speakers bureau. You could lecture about the importance of our country and others partnering for the greater good of all people."

Justin pulled out his PDA and wrote down what he'd just said. "You'd get paid an honorarium to travel to different women's groups, sharing advice—"

"On how to be the perfect hostess?" Cheryl turned on the lights in their bedroom. "I'm glad we talked."

Cheryl unbuttoned her blouse at the wrist and shook her head at him. Justin didn't speak as she walked into her closet and exited moments later in a long cotton robe. She was naked underneath.

She'd put on heeled slippers with white fur at the top, making her legs look undeniably sexy.

Justin wanted her so badly he physically hurt.

"What do you think?" he asked, then wished he hadn't. For the first time in their relationship, he couldn't tell her thoughts by the expression on her face.

"I'm going to take a shower."

"Me too," he said, before she closed her bathroom door.

Before he'd realized what he'd done, Justin was outside the door of her bathroom. He caught himself. Cheryl had made it clear a long time ago that she didn't want his company in her bathroom. She probably didn't now. Not even when he wanted her with the hunger of a teenager facing his first bare breast.

Justin's cell phone rang and he snatched it from his pocket. "Justin Crawford."

"Ambassador, Tommy Ahern here." The senator sounded very much like the good ol' boy he was. "Do you have a couple minutes? I'd like to bend yo' ear."

Justin's gaze swung to the closed door. "Sure, Senator. What can I do for you?"

"Congratulations, the preliminaries on your background check came back clean as a whistle."

"That fast?"

"You haven't been far and wide, so it's been relatively easy. I'd tell you if we'd found something that we couldn't work with. We've about got all our eggs in your basket."

Justin knew better than that. "I'm honored. What can I do for you, sir?"

"Have you formed your committee yet?"

"Sir, we just met this morning."

Tommy laughed. "That so? Seems like we've been at this for a long while. I guess you're right. Well, I might be gettin' ahead of myself, but I've got a campaign manager that's a shark in a skirt. She's been around the campaign block many times. Name's Amy Shaw. Heard of her?"

"Of course. She worked on both presidential campaigns. Democratic and Republican." Justin recalled that the second administration had taken some flack from that decision, but after they'd won, everybody called their strategy brilliant.

"She was the creator of the expression 'the hanging chad,' then after the election she dropped out of sight. Some time back, I'd heard that she threatened to make it her life's work to abolish the electoral college if the government didn't get its act together regarding voting."

"You are correct." Tommy didn't sound as enthused as he'd been a moment ago. "Her talents are better spent helping eager young people such as yo'self get into office. I'd like for you to talk to her, if you have time."

Tommy phrased his statement as a request, but Justin didn't get the impression that he was being given a choice. His first instinct was to say no, but a knee-jerk reaction could come back to kick him down the road.

"Tommy, I don't mind meeting with her, but I'll be selecting my own committee."

" 'Course you will," Tommy said loudly, although Justin still heard the shower cut off. "Nine o'clock at the law offices of Jacobs and Sternheart. They're downtown. Good night."

Justin put the PDA phone on silent and set it down on Cheryl's desk before heading to his bathroom to shower.

He and Cheryl used to shower together all the time. With their current arrangement, he hadn't been underwater with her in years.

How was that possible? Especially since she had this new body? Justin forced his brain elsewhere. She'd listened to him tonight. At times he'd felt a real connection between them as he'd shared his dreams.

Her ultimatum had been a cry for attention and he'd answered. And he would again tonight until she'd had enough.

The shower spray turned into fiery hot needles, and he struggled to adjust the flow. Hands overhead, as he twisted the nozzle, one of the heads came off in his palm. Hot water poured out on him, until he was able to wrench the nozzle into the off position.

Justin left the shower stall. He examined the head, the washer, and the pipe. Nothing seemed wrong with them, but still he left them on the sink, making a mental note to call the repairman in the morning. Yanking a towel from the warmer, he dried his face, gentle on his shoulders and back, which had taken the brunt of the near-scalding water.

He looked like a lobster.

He brushed his teeth and tossed his clothes into the dry-cleaning bag before heading back to their room.

"Hey," he said, noticing that Cheryl was in bed reading. "Do we have anything for a burn?"

"What's burned?"

He turned around. "My back."

She scrambled out of bed, took a look, and hurried to the bathroom. "How'd that happen?"

"The water was too hot so I tried to adjust the spray."

"Sit down," she said, climbing onto the bed behind him. "I'd better get Mr. Gonzalez over here to check the pressure," she said, massaging his back with gentle hands.

"I can check the pressure," he told her.

Her hands slowed. "You? Sure. Okay."

"What's that mean? *Sure. Okay.* I'm a man. I can check the water pressure in my own damned house."

Cheryl's breath caressed his back and neck while her hands played with his lower back. "I don't know why you're so sensitive, Justin."

"I'm not sensitive," he said, the front of his towel adjusting each time her silky pajamas grazed his back. "Except when my wife challenges my manhood."

"I did no such thing. Mr. Gonzalez has taken care of this house since it was built. You're done."

"There's more."

She looked around his shoulder at him, her face skeptical. "I don't see anymore."

"My whole backside got burned."

"I'm not touching your butt. Forget it." She fixed the lid on the jar of cream and massaged the rest into her hands.

Justin leaned back on his elbow, his head propped up on his hand. "What do you have against my backside?"

"Nothing."

The pulse in her neck jumped and Justin wanted to leap also. She might have been trying to act indifferent, but her body gave her away.

After having made love to her hundreds of time, he knew her hot spots.

Cheryl had been kneeling, but now her legs were stretched out, her feet crossed at the ankles, less than twelve inches from his face.

"Remember when we were in college, and you fell off your bike while trying to avoid that car? Your ankle was messed up. Was it this one?"

He gently separated her feet and, with just enough pressure to let her know he wasn't letting go, perused her right ankle, dragging his thumb along the inside bone. "It was scraped badly. Broken, we later found out." He pressed his lips to that bone, the sole of her foot on his abs.

Her toes crinkled in his chest, and he licked until her leg shuddered. "You were in a cast—"

"Six weeks," she said, gently tugging her foot.

"You had to learn to walk again."

"Yeah." Cheryl sighed as his lips curved around her big toe. He took a sensual bite. As his lips danced over her four remaining toes, Justin could feel his sex find the path to light and peek out.

"Every day we'd go for a walk." His hand around her calf, he moved up her leg, his mouth claiming her, one bite at a time. "Our goal, that old oak tree."

Cheryl had leaned back on her hands, her elbows locked straight, her thighs rigid. "Every day you took me farther," she said, picking up his lead on the story.

Justin separated the hem of the silky robe from her short nightie and glimpsed the channel to ecstasy. He lifted her leg and took a bite from the curve between calf and thigh.

Cheryl jumped and her legs unlocked.

He pushed her leg farther down his body, her toes dancing with his sex, his mouth on the path to claiming hers.

"And you'd kiss me longer each time."

"Like this?" Justin kissed the inside of one thigh, then the other.

"On the lips," she said, in the soft southern drawl she'd abandoned years ago.

With her leg up, Justin took the familiar route. His lips closed over her intimate folds and she arched into his kiss. "Not there," she whispered.

He pulled her to him, claimed her with his tongue first, then his lips. "Oh yes," she groaned, "there."

Justin closed his eyes, making love to her with his mouth, and listened to the only woman he'd ever loved reach her sexual peak, and when she began to slide, he entered her, making her climax again.

Justin didn't care what anyone else said, when it came to making love, he thought the missionary position was the best.

He loved the way she breathed his name, the taste of her skin, the smell of their two bodies in heat, the dual feelings of her knotted breasts taut against his chest, her nails running from his butt to his neck.

But what had him addicted was watching her climax.

Over the years Cheryl had become this polished, perfect politician's wife, never a hair out of place, never an imperfect emotion.

But in bed, he got off on knowing that only he had touched her in ways that made her hair wild, her eyes smoky, her voice hoarse, her skin wet, and her mouth foul. In bed, he loved for her to tell him to fuck her.

Suddenly his wife flipped them, her body astride his, their lips tight. She'd become a lioness, and he sought to extinguish her every insatiable desire.

The twist in their raw coupling rushed him to meet her passion. Justin tried to slow down, but with Cheryl bouncing in his lap, coherent thoughts slipped away like droplets of sweat.

"Do you love me?" she asked, her eyes stormy.

"You know I do."

Her legs tightened on him, and the shift in control widened. "Say it," she urged.

Justin didn't want to give in, and tried to psyche himself out.

Cheryl's head fell sideways and her eyes closed as her fingers dug into his shoulders. Their bodies slapped and as each thrust took them closer to the pinnacle, he knew he was closer than he wanted to be. She had to go over first, then he'd see her satisfaction and know that if she felt this comfortable yielding to him so intimately, she'd be his forever.

He tried to flip her, but Cheryl's heat tightened, as she clasped his face in her hands and kissed him hard. "Say it," she ground out, her body turning his into one massive erogenous zone.

He reached down and she trapped his fingers between her abs and his. With Cheryl on top of him, Justin felt his control slip with each dip of her hips against his.

Holding her rear, he sat up and pushed deeper, her shoulders drawing back until her body was in a perfect arch.

Her whimpers signified how close she was to exploding, and Justin quickened the pace. As release swirled around his feet, Justin whispered the words "I love you."

Cheryl's body hit his with such intensity he fell backward, taking her with him.

Then she cheated. Her heat gripped him like a glove and his body started to take the leap. The more he fought, the faster the bittersweet rush of ecstasy ran to greet him.

For the first time, he was going over without her.

Her eyes begged for something and Justin tried to obliterate the request. He'd seen the distant question there for about a year, and he stopped wondering how to answer.

When she pressed down on him, he dropped his hands between them and found what he sought.

Cheryl's cry of surprise evolved into a scream as she moved against him once more, sending him over before she joined him on the zigzagging ride to paradise.

Eleven

Cheryl hugged her side of the bed, the mattress her anchor and her prison. How could she have done this to herself again? She'd vowed to stop making love with Justin to get his attention, but just the opposite had happened.

Her body had betrayed her mind again, leaving her powerless to his touch.

Now she hoped he was asleep. She had to get out of the room in order to clear her head.

Guilt that she wasn't being true to herself swarmed through her body and Cheryl knew that she'd come to a pivotal point in her life. Either she stood up for herself, or she had to accept the role she'd assumed twenty years ago. Her heart revolted and a war raged inside her chest.

Teaching in Africa had taken on a significance she hadn't expected. Ideas swirled in her head about the lessons she planned to share with the women, while the other part of her could only imagine what she'd learn from them.

Yesterday, before the funeral and the baby, she'd spoken to a former classmate who'd earned her medical degree and doctorate in molecular biology.

Now she was a researcher for a major drug company, and she'd just joined the lecture circuit. Not that Cheryl needed money, but her friend earned a healthy salary and had the respect of scholars and students worldwide. Cheryl was envious.

Dr. Babomunda had given Cheryl a reading list of material on the South African culture, and she planned to order every book in order to enhance her knowledge.

This was her time. She'd felt alive and important. Until she'd arrived at the Norths' home and seen her husband in action.

Justin had been attentive to Lea and Sam, stepping into the role of a good family friend with ease.

Cheryl had tried several times to get his attention, even entering a conversation he'd been involved in, but after she'd spoken he didn't even make a supportive comment. The worst part of the entire exchange happened when she tried to kiss him.

Justin had turned his head so quickly she ended up kissing his throat. Not what she'd intended or expected. She'd given him space after that, hoping that she hadn't become relegated to the position of an afterthought.

For two hours she'd visited with acquaintances, catching up on news from the States, until the group began to disperse and head home. She'd searched for Justin, but when she didn't find him she left. Loneliness followed her home and took up court in her heart.

Jett had college. Justin, politics.

What did she have?

Me. Teaching. Support from family and friends. Goals, dreams.

Now as she lay in bed beside the man she'd pledged to love until the day she died, Cheryl knew there was only one right thing to do.

She couldn't make love to Justin again. And since she couldn't trust herself not to succumb, she'd have to leave their bedroom.

Now that the decision had been made, Cheryl felt her spirit ease and her mind flow into a restful state.

She had the right to pursue her dreams, and she had a right to expect that her husband would fulfill his promise.

She hoped sex was the only thing she and Justin would have to lose before they got their act together.

The phone shook her from sleep, but Cheryl didn't move to answer it. So few people knew she was home, it probably wasn't for her anyway. Justin crawled out of bed, the small handset to his ear, and left the bedroom.

Typical, she thought, turning flat on her back. What would he do if the phone had never been invented? *Invent it*, she told herself as she tried to make up her mind about what she'd do today.

The door to their bedroom opened and she sealed her eyes shut. If he touched her, she'd submit. Especially on her back as she was now. It wouldn't take much for him to have her body just the way he liked her. Wet and accepting.

The bedroom door closed and her head snapped up. What had he been doing in there if he didn't want to make love?

Her eyes adjusted to the dim light from the closet door. He'd left something on her desk, but she couldn't make it out through the sheer curtain around the bed.

Cheryl hurried to her desk and slipped the note from Justin's richly textured personal stationery.

> *Cheryl, I'm ready to retire. Meet me at the Hilton on Courtland Street at four o'clock so that we can plan our future. Love, Justin.*

Yes, thank you, God.

Fully awake now, Cheryl glided into her closet, looking for something thrilling and sexy. Justin had finally come around and he deserved a reward. Something decadent, for his eyes only. A white body stocking caught her attention, and Cheryl tried it on. She'd wear it, under a Dolce and Gabana suit, but when he unwrapped the plain but tasteful wrapper, he'd find pure sin.

They would have tremendous sex, she predicted, any way he wanted.

Her heart swelled as she thought of the sacrifice Justin would make to leave his post as ambassador.

Maybe the grant had been approved! Perhaps that's why he had felt he couldn't leave the post and join her in Africa.

Tonight they'd have a lot to celebrate. And she'd plan a fabulous retirement party.

Changing into her robe, Cheryl opened her PDA and within the hour had an intimate party planned for the entire family.

She dialed Keisha.

"Morning," Keisha said, sounding groggy.

"He's retiring."

"Get out!" Keisha's voice bounced through the phone lines, now fully awake.

"Nope." Cheryl grinned. "I'm so relieved and relaxed."

"Oooo. I think Julian was going to break a world record over here last night."

Cheryl blushed. "Making love?"

"Yep. What about you two?"

The silk robe and sex talk made her remember every time he'd entered her, the intense expression on his face. His commands for her to climax. Her pleasure in obliging.

"We made love like we were newlyweds. Listen, I've got a full day ahead. We're going to meet at the Hilton downtown. I planned an intimate retirement party."

"Justin had better be thankful for you. You're an amazing wife."

"You say that because I learned from you."

"That's true, but you're a gem. How about this? Would you mind if I got a congratulations cake for you?"

The idea thrilled Cheryl, but she didn't want to steal Justin's glory.

"Keisha, we can wait until it's closer to the time for me to leave."

"Cheryl, I'm getting you a cake. This is a big deal and you don't have to let him have this moment alone. While one door closes, another opens."

"Okay," she said. "I'd love it."

"Have you called everyone yet?"

"Not yet."

"Let me do that for you. I'll call Jett too."

"Thanks, Keisha. Now I can get my hair done in peace."

"Where and when?"

"The Hilton downtown, four o'clock. See you later."

"Sweetie, I'm happy for you."

"Me too. Bye."

Cheryl fell on her back and kicked her feet with joy, laughing hysterically.

Suddenly her day went from relaxing to super busy. She hurried to the bedroom door.

"Justin? Justin?" she called, ready to start the celebration. They could shower together . . . she'd light candles . . .

Silence greeted her. She bit her lip and didn't allow disappointment to creep into her joy. Today was going to be the best. Justin would be thrilled and so would her family. Cheryl hurriedly dialed her mother and father, but no one answered.

Her brow crinkled. Where were her parents at this hour? Country folk were up at dawn, and her family was the epitome of country. Now that her mom and dad were retired, they traveled a good bit, but always let her know when they were on the road.

She left a message on their voice mail, then dialed their cell phone. Her mother answered after one ring. "Mama, is everything all right?"

"Bill, it's Cheryl. Yes, darlin', me and Daddy are fine. How are you?"

Cheryl laughed, relieved. "Fine, Mama. Where are you? I just called the house, and nobody answered."

"Bill, she wants to know where we're at. Darlin', we're out and about. Just trying to get some exercise. Yo' daddy's got a gut on him since he retired."

This time Cheryl smirked. Her mother was the fat one of the pair. "Mama, I want you and Daddy to come to Atlanta. Justin and I are home for a few days, and I have a big announcement."

"Bill, she wants us to come to Atlanta."

Cheryl shook her head. All of her life, her mother had never been able to hold a conversation without repeating everything to her husband. Cheryl recalled how her friends used to think that her father was hard of hearing.

"Tell her okay. We'll meet her at the house, but we're going to have to stay over tonight because I'm not driving back in the dark. What time?"

"Daddy says okay."

"Mama, meet us at the Hilton on Courtland Street. We're going to do something special. Four o'clock," Cheryl said loudly, saving her mother from having to repeat. "I love you, Daddy. Love you, Mama."

"We love you too, darlin'. See you later."

Cheryl ran luxuriously warm bathwater and sank into it.

For the first time in a long time they'd be Mr.

and Mrs. Crawford. No titles, no positions, no duties, no responsibilities, nobody rushing them to do something or to be somewhere else. They'd be regular. Like they'd been in the beginning.

They could fall in love all over again. They had sixty days until they were to leave for Africa. Falling in love the first time hadn't taken that long. She stretched her toes, remembering how they'd loved each other with an abandon that had been breathtaking and endearing.

Justin used to kiss her then—not just in bed, where he could make her open up to feelings she couldn't ever show the world, but anywhere. In the car, in church, at school, or in a restaurant full of people.

He'd get real close, and he'd kind of half pucker, half smile. His eyelids would be lowered, black lashes shielding to-die-for eyes, then he'd tilt his chin, and say, "Kiss."

Cheryl drew her hand up between her legs and a warm flush flooded her body. Her fingers were not nearly as long and as effective as Justin's, but her body responded to the stroking by supplying a steady beat.

She loved when his mouth would be against hers, his hands driving her into an out-of-body experience. Justin had impeccable timing. He'd wait until she was about to explode and would seal her mouth with a delicious kiss, as his fingers navigated her trip to the stars.

"Cheryl?" Justin's voice boomed out at her.

She yelped and nearly jumped out of the tub. "Yes?"

The real estate agent that had sold them the

house had touted the attributes of having a built-in intercom. Cheryl was sure it was her least favorite feature.

"You okay?" he asked.

"Yes," she said, draping one leg, then the other over the tub. She wrapped herself in a bath sheet. "Just getting a bath. Where were you? I called you a while ago."

"I'd already left, but I forgot some papers. I don't have time to run upstairs. When we meet later, can you bring my blue Hugo Boss tie with you?" he asked.

"Sure, darlin'. Anything else?" she said, her heart swelling with love.

"Just you."

She smiled and walked over to the wall unit. "Why don't you come upstairs?" She looked at the tub of water, glad she'd already gotten started. "Ten minutes tops, I promise."

His chuckle made her legs feel like spaghetti. "I can't. I'm late for a meeting with Ross. Got to run. Bye."

"Bye," she said.

Cheryl hurried to the window knowing that in a few seconds Justin's Lincoln would swoop from the side of the house, and she'd see it for a brief second before it hit the street.

He barely hesitated before pulling out onto the main road and driving out of sight.

A teardrop sound interrupted her window gazing, and she picked up her PDA.

Jett was going to meet them at the Hilton for dinner. He was bringing Kathy.

Cheryl began nourishing her body with cream, counting her blessings.

Today she'd get her husband back, Jett was joining them with his new girlfriend, and her parents were coming to town.

Everyone would be thrilled with her news, and she would be sure to make Justin feel special. Resigning his post as ambassador was a huge step, but Justin had definitely come around. He'd been honorable, and while being true to one's word didn't require a reward, Cheryl wanted to make him feel like a king.

Why was Justin meeting with their accountant? she wondered, pulling on stockings. Probably getting their financial business in order now that they'd be moving to Africa.

Just the thought thrilled and excited her. Africa. The mother country. The beginning of civilization. The land of kings and queens. Nelson Mandela and Bishop Desmond Tutu had once been guests of Pops Crawford. Cheryl had been honored to share their presence.

Two years ago she'd known so little about Africa and its people, but now that she was going, her thirst for knowledge was insatiable.

As little as she knew, Cheryl was certain of one thing. She was already in love with the continent, and she would do everything in her power to help her husband adjust.

Suddenly she couldn't wait to see him, and let him know how much she loved him.

Twelve

"You could win the Senate race, if you do what I say."

Justin listened intently to campaign manager Amy Shaw. The five-foot-eleven blue-eyed blond woman from Kansas City, Kansas, wasn't what he'd expected. He'd seen her on CNN during the last campaign but she'd been considerably heavier, and without as nice a disposition. He wondered about her turnabout, but then disregarded the thought. He wanted to win the Senate race. Nothing else mattered unless it was going to help him achieve that goal.

"What would you suggest?"

"You have to be someone the public believes will listen to them, get the job done, and not be a lying crook. And they want you to have a great personal life and they don't care how you achieve it."

He shrugged. "My personal life is just fine."

"But you lack statewide name recognition. Helping you achieve that is one of my stronger roles, and one that will be critical for your campaign manager to have."

"What is your strongest asset?" he asked, hoping to flap the unflappable woman.

"Winning."

He gave a curt nod. "What type of team would you recommend me choosing?"

"You'll need a financial manager, publicist, various coordinators to manage volunteers, fund-raisers, and so on, and a superb administrative assistant. However, one of the most important support people on your team will be your wife. Where is she, by the way?"

Taken aback at the abrupt question, Justin took a few seconds before he responded. He'd tried to call her an hour ago, but she'd been at the hairdresser. He'd intentionally not asked Cheryl to attend this meeting.

Announcing his retirement from being an ambassador was a big step. But he hadn't found the words to tell her of his decision.

"Will this happen often?"

"I beg your pardon, Ms. Shaw?"

"Ambassador, if you're going to get testy at a question as insignificant as the whereabouts of your wife, how are you going to field questions about your racial preference?"

"Why would anyone ask questions about that? My wife is black."

"But I'm not. And people will resent me as your campaign manager unless you and Mrs. Crawford set the tone. If she's visible and campaigning for you, then there's no problem when you and I make appearances."

Again, Amy had raised a good point. When he and Cheryl had talked, there was no direct mention of her supporting him. Justin had taken it for granted that she would.

Last night, she'd advised him to follow his dream. She hadn't said anything about *her* following *his* dream.

But she seemed amenable to the idea of mentoring a young girl, and joining the speakers' bureau for spouses of senators.

Discomfort swelled inside him and Justin wished he could dislodge it. Cheryl's stubborn streak had reared its head and he'd tried to diffuse it by making passionate love to her. Except, she'd flipped the script and he'd peaked ahead of her. A first in their marriage, especially since he'd always initiated lovemaking and made sure he'd taken care of her first.

Cheryl seemed to have come into her own and realized her inner strength. She'd taken an ordinary passionate night of lovemaking, and burned it into his brain forever.

To anyone else, that might seem insignificant, but to Justin, the shift in their roles had been enough to keep him awake long after she'd fallen asleep.

"Mr. Crawford?"

Justin jerked. "I'm sorry. Please continue, Ms. Shaw."

"Call me Shaw. You're a busy man," she acknowledged, her voice edged with warning. "I won't take up too much more of your time."

"Not a problem."

"I only work with couples, Ambassador. That way our entire focus is on the campaign and not your marital issues. I don't do messy situations."

"Our marriage is intact," Justin said defensively.

She smiled. "Good, because there'll be no girlfriends, boy toys, psychics, parents, siblings, or mothers-in-law. During the campaign, I'll be in charge of getting you elected and that means no go-betweens. Sometimes I'll be your best friend and other times your worst enemy, but you stand a good chance of winning if I'm on your side. I don't want any problems with your wife, Ambassador. That's why I asked for this meeting with both of you. If she's out of commission now, how can you be sure she's not out doing something that will hurt your campaign later?"

Justin didn't know. Especially now. His suspicions weren't new. Ever since he found out she'd gone to Puerto Rico without telling him, Justin had been on edge.

The new body, new attitude, and now Cheryl's new sexual prowess. Was she having an affair? If he'd asked the question a year ago, he'd have said no without hesitating. But today was different. Yet Justin felt the need to protect her.

"My wife is devoted to me and no one else," he said, coolly.

"Have you ever slipped, Ambassador? Had an illicit something on the side? Maybe a one-night stand you don't want to remember? Maybe with the beautiful girl next door, Lea North?"

Justin had heard that Amy Shaw was tough, but he hadn't been told she was crass.

"Lea and I have been friends since our freshman year in college. Her husband became one of my best friends. I fell in love with my wife twenty years ago, and since then I've never touched another woman. Nothing will happen between me and anyone else besides Cheryl. Are we clear?"

When she smiled, he realized he'd just been tested again.

"Good answer. Ambassador, women from the past will come out of the woodwork making accusations of infidelity, advances, and sexual encounters that may or may not have happened. I just wanted you to get a taste of what's to come."

"I'm not worried about that. My staff is loyal and I've treated them well, but never improperly."

"Your opponent will try to discredit you, but if you have nothing to hide, there'll be nothing to find. I've helped two presidents, ten senators, and three congressmen win office. In the packet I've included my references, the budget you'll need, and other essentials. This is a big investment, but worth it."

"I want to win."

"I haven't lost one yet."

"You're hired."

"I'll schedule a press conference."

"Beat you to it. How's today at four o'clock at the Hilton?"

"Soon but doable. I'd better get started. I'll need a check for two hundred fifty thousand dollars."

"I'll need a good reason to give it to you."

She gazed at him. "I don't work half-assed. I get my money up front, and to get you established I need capital. We can go over logistics tonight, but I need my check before we get started."

"No problem." He wrote the check and gave it to her.

"Very good. After the press conference, we'll strategize, and then I'll meet your wife and the rest of your family."

"See you later."

Justin waited for Shaw to leave and wondered if he liked her. She had an impressive record and the men she'd helped get into office had long-standing careers, but her in-your-face attitude could get old. And for Justin, that didn't sit well.

He dialed his house and when Cheryl didn't answer he left a voice mail on her cell phone. "Cheryl, it's me. Wondering where you are. Give me a call right away."

Justin hung up and dialed his office in Ecuador. He hadn't talked to Maura in twenty-four hours.

"Hey, boss," she said. "How's it going?"

"I've got news."

"What's going on?" She sounded so morbid that Justin prolonged the suspense.

"I wish I were there to tell you, but the timing is off."

"It's not you and Mrs. Crawford, is it?"

He pressed the phone into his ear. "Why would you ask that?"

"No reason." Maura didn't elaborate.

"Tell me."

"Sir, I don't feel comfortable delving into your personal business. Was there something you needed from me?"

"The truth," he said, growing angry. "Now! Or someone will be looking for a job."

She gurgled a bit. "Would you really fire me?"

Justin wouldn't. He needed Maura. She knew how he liked things done. That's why he'd transferred her to Ecuador. "I'd think about it," he said, hoping she'd take him seriously.

"Chad left."

"Where'd he go?"

"To Atlanta."

Justin sat forward. "Why? I thought he was working on the grant. He was supposed to attend a meeting in my place at the embassy."

"It was canceled. Two of the directors got ill from food poisoning. Nothing serious, but they delayed the meeting for two days. Chad is in Atlanta. If you haven't seen him, then that's good."

"Why is that?"

"I'm uncomfortable—"

"So is unemployment," he threatened.

"He thinks he's in love with Mrs. Crawford."

Justin didn't realize he was walking around until he bumped his knee on the file cabinet. "What did you say?"

"Please don't make me repeat it. It's been going on for six months."

"An affair," he breathed, his throat closing.

"No. As far as I know she hasn't returned his advances. In fact she told him she was in love with you. But men in love . . . Look, I've got calls waiting. I thought you said you had something to tell me."

"I'm going to be running for Dan North's Senate seat. Maura, I'll call you back."

Justin hung up, grabbed his keys, then stopped. He dialed home and waited for the housekeeper to answer. "Mrs. Crane, do you know where my wife is?"

"She's getting her hair done, then meeting you this afternoon. Shall I try to contact her?"

"No," he said, feeling foolish. Of course she wouldn't cheat on him.

Chad being in love with his wife was a problem, but not one he had to deal with now.

"Thank you," he said and hung up.

He dialed Chad's cell phone, but he didn't pick up. The bastard. Justin wanted to hunt him down and teach him a lesson, but he was meeting with his accountant in thirty minutes.

Chad didn't know whom he was messing with. He redialed the number.

"Chad, Justin Crawford here. You're fired, and if I find out you've been with my wife, you'll regret it for the rest of your miserable life."

Thirteen

Justin sat in the thirtieth-floor restaurant of the Hilton Hotel, the lone customer. The view of Atlanta from this vantage point revealed a thriving city, one that attracted dreamers who imagined better lives for themselves and their families.

How do I reach them?

"Anything else to drink, sir?" Juancarlo asked, a silver coffeepot in hand.

"No, thanks." Justin gestured for him not to leave. "How long have you been working today?"

"Nine hours. Why?" he asked.

"Just wondering what people have to do to make a living in this town."

"You are out of work?"

"Between assignments," Justin said with a smile.

"You're a sharp dresser and you've got money to back you up. You won't be unemployed long."

"Why do you say that?"

"Your suit is very expensive, but your watch gave you away."

Juancarlo smiled and Justin nodded.

"You were born here. You speak the language. If you need a social program, you know how to find one. Not like many Mexicans. We heard about living in Georgia, about the good school systems, and the fact that there was work. My friends and I had to work years to save up enough money to be brought over, or we risked our lives sneaking over. When we got here, we got any job so we could start making money. Real money to buy things people take for granted."

"You mean blacks?" Justin asked, intrigued that they were having such an honest exchange.

"Everyone," Juancarlo said. "Here, people take money for granted. The furniture that is cast off, the clothes that are discarded, the food that is thrown away, especially in the food service business." He shook his head. "I see that, sometimes it makes me want to cry when I think of families at home that truly have nothing."

"You're an educated man. Why do you work here, Juancarlo?"

"Because I'm illegal," he said with pride. "I've applied to become a citizen, but the process takes a long time."

"Do you have a second job?"

"Yes. The first job is so that I can stay here in the U.S., and the second one is so my family can stay alive at home."

"You're going to make it, Juancarlo." Justin offered his hand and they shook.

"Thank you. I've got to get back to work."

Justin settled down again, but his mind stuck on Juancarlo's words. He knew he was privileged and he hadn't ever taken that for granted.

He pulled out the notes from his lunch with

Ross. They'd spent the better part of their meeting running figures for the campaign.

According to Shaw, he'd have to contribute from his own personal funds close to a million dollars. Fund-raising, he was told, couldn't be his emphasis with only six weeks until the election. He'd have to make money while crisscrossing the state, winning over voters.

He also needed a staff and a facility for a headquarters, so after today's press conference, he'd have to hit the ground running.

He and Cheryl had the money, but according to Ross he'd be using roughly half of their total savings. And that didn't leave a lot left over.

By giving Shaw the green light, he'd dropped a quarter million today alone. Ross had cautioned him to talk to Cheryl first, but he hadn't and hindsight was nagging him now. Hopefully she'd come to understand later. But today might be a little rough.

His phone rang. "Justin Crawford."

"Shaw here," she responded. "Have you made any decisions about the first fifteen items on the list I provided?"

There wasn't anything soft or fuzzy about this woman. He tried to ignore her abrupt nature and focused on the agenda.

"Go ahead with two through ten. Before today is over, I'll make a decision about the facility."

"You're doing this backward. There's no need for me to initialize phone service if there's no installation site. You need a campaign headquarters first. I gave you three choices, sir, you need to pick one."

"Shaw, trust me. My family owns property all over this state. I won't pay rent before checking with them. I'll make a decision before the end of the day."

"Your call," she said. "We'll talk later about staff. I've got calls to make before the press conference. How are you feeling? Confident? Unsure? Can I help you with your speech?"

"I feel great and no, the speech you provided is just fine."

Shaw laughed. "You're the first candidate that's ever read it."

"That's good to know," he said, mildly surprised. The speech was very good. "See you later," Justin told her, grinning.

"Righto," she said and hung up.

The second call wasn't as easy, but after talking to the president's second assistant, he waited nearly an hour before the president came on the line.

He congratulated Justin, accepted his resignation, and offered to make a stop on his own campaign route so they could talk. They agreed and hung up.

Justin completed his calls, then consulted his watch. By the time he got downstairs, the press as well as his family would be arriving.

He knew his plan was risky and not without significant problems, but this was the opportunity of a lifetime.

An hour later at the press conference, Justin entered the room. His wife and son, his parents, brothers, their wives and children were in attendance, along with the press. Shaw hovered on the periphery.

Even Cheryl's folks had accepted his invitation to come to Atlanta to celebrate the big surprise announcement.

As the reporters set up and tested their lights, Justin reviewed the three-by-five cards in his pocket.

"You know these backward and forward." Shaw removed them from his hand. "Be yourself. That tie isn't working. Randall," she called quietly into a tiny headset that lined her jaw in thin clear plastic. "Bring the eagle the red and blue."

Justin puffed up a little. He was the eagle.

"I had my wife bring me a tie. Cheryl," he said, marveling at the body he hadn't realized she possessed. She glided toward him, her navy suit accenting her figure. Could he ever love another man?

"Yes, darling?" She'd left her parents, who smiled and waved. Cheryl's body pressed against his for a brief, nonverbal hello.

"My tie," he said.

"Right here."

She removed the designer silk from her bag, where she'd rolled it into a cotton handkerchief. Cheryl gingerly handled the tie, and as he slipped off the first one she draped his neck with the other.

He regarded her mouth as she fixed his collar. She had beautiful thick lips, lined, colored, and glossed to perfection. But he liked her mouth most when it was naked and yielding. When

Cheryl kissed him, she put her heart into it and would wind her arms around his neck and drag him close. Her kisses were so wanton, they had the power to undo every level of professionalism he'd learned and strip him down to the essence of his manhood.

He used to growl when he knew she was moving in for the kill, and the few times his brothers had been around and heard him, they would tease him mercilessly.

He had to stop thinking of kissing her. Only Cheryl could make him lose focus in a meeting full of politicians. Had one of his wife's most desirable features been pressed against another man's mouth, chest, sex? If Chad loved her, did she share his affection?

For the briefest second Justin wondered if he'd failed Cheryl. If he'd somehow not provided her with what she needed to be happy. The idea mystified him. He gripped her hand.

"What is it, Justin?"

He wanted her right then, but that was his masculinity talking, not his brain. He wouldn't have her again—he wagered—for some time. At least not until she got over being angry.

Justin placed a bet with himself that Cheryl would come around to his way of thinking.

He hoped he was right.

Shaw stood a few feet away, watching them intently.

"You look wonderful." Justin slid his hand up Cheryl's side.

"You look pretty good yourself, for an old retired man." She took his face between her hands

and made him look at her. "Don't look so petri-
fied. We're doing the right thing, love."

The pit in his stomach grew into a pothole.

Shaw watched the byplay and gave a nod of approval. While Justin changed, Cheryl introduced
herself.

"I'm Cheryl Crawford."

"Call me Shaw. You will stand on the left of the
candidate. When he steps forward to speak, you
stand one foot to his left, six inches back. At this
position the wife photographs well. You won't
speak, but at the end of the announcement, you
may join the candidate but only if given the go by
me."

"Who are you again? I must have missed something."

Justin gave Shaw a warning look and steered
Cheryl away from what could have been an ex-
plosive situation. "Shaw works for me," he said,
and glanced at his watch before taking her hand.

"What's she here for?"

"Transition," he said, walking toward the
podium as people began to applaud. He spotted
Lea North and waved. Shaw didn't miss a beat
and headed toward the widow.

Justin took his position at the microphone and
waited as his family assembled behind him.

Cheryl stood off to the side and seemed about
to disappear when he snagged her hand and
brought it to his lips.

"I guess it's my turn to tell you not to look so
scared," he said.

"I've been set up."

The haunting words tore him up inside.

Flashbulbs popped.

"I hoped you'd understand."

"I don't."

Cheryl's eyes gleamed and he wanted to rewind time and go down the road called trust. But he couldn't. Any more than he could erase the furious expression on Jett's face.

The microphones were live when he turned to the crowd.

"Good afternoon and thank you for joining me. I know you'd like nothing better than to get into rush-hour traffic in the next half hour, so I'll keep this short."

The members of the press and several members of his political party laughed.

"Don't do this," Cheryl whispered.

The agony in her voice ate into his conscience until he lost his train of thought. "Today . . . This afternoon, I'd like to announce that after a great deal of thought and contemplation, I have decided to resign my post as ambassador to Ecuador. My family has come to love the people and the country, and we are sorely going to miss both. But wherever there is a little cloudiness, there is also a silver lining."

"If you love me . . ." Cheryl said from behind him.

"Uh . . ." he said, looking out over the crowd of people gathered. *Stay focused.* "Senator Dan North had been a dear friend of mine since college. Several days ago, a father, husband, and community leader was called Home, leaving us all to come to grips with his death. And though we will probably never understand why he was taken so soon, I believe that Dan would want his work continued here in Georgia and across this nation."

"Justin, don't," Cheryl hissed.

"He wouldn't want the work he'd begun to go unfinished because of his death. That is why, after talking with Lea and many members of both parties, I have decided to run for Dan's vacant Senate seat."

Lea North walked up and kissed Justin's cheek. She took the microphone but didn't speak, allowing him to have his moment. Lea's presence gave him full endorsement.

With the steady, bright lights from TV cameras glaring up at him, Justin felt a great rush of relief.

People applauded and shouted questions, and Justin turned and motioned his family forward.

Only, when he looked into his son's face he saw unmitigated fury.

Justin turned to reach for Cheryl, but she was gone.

Fourteen

Footsteps hounded Cheryl as she race-walked through the lobby. Was that her pride being pounded into dust or was someone actually following her? Both, she realized.

"Mrs. Crawford, why'd you leave the press conference? Aren't you a supporter of your husband? Will you vote for him on election day?"

Cheryl tried to get to the elevator and away from the reporter. The suite she'd reserved for the family's party would be a temporary refuge, but she had to get away from the prying eyes of this man before she broke. She hated this part of being a public figure almost as much as the actual job itself.

Tears pressed against the back of her eyelids, but she wouldn't let them fall. Not in front of this ridiculous reporter who wouldn't give her enough room to make her escape unnoticed. Cheryl finally stopped moving.

"Why'd you leave? Trouble in paradise?" he asked.

"No."

The man perspired from exertion, his garlic-heavy breath flapping the paper he wrote on. She tried to hold her breath, but her lungs moved too rapidly. She felt as if she were hyperventilating.

"Then explain your quick and embarrassing departure."

My husband is a liar. He makes promises he won't keep. Don't vote for Justin Crawford, he isn't a man of his word.

Cheryl wondered could she really out him. Could she ruin Justin's campaign and any hopes of a political career with a couple sentences?

With her stomach tied in knots, she knew she couldn't betray Justin. Despite her fury and her pain, she couldn't tell the world what a first-class jerk he was. Her stomach twisted and she gripped her belly until the cramp passed.

The reporter stepped back as if she had the plague. "You're sick."

Cheryl nodded. "Stomach virus." She coughed in his direction and he scrambled as if her germs wouldn't thwart his obscene attempt to avoid them.

"After I visit the ladies' room, perhaps we could finish our interview?" she asked, coughing delicately into her hand, then offered to shake his.

"No!" He shoved his pad into his pocket. "There's no story here," he said, and walked off, mumbling.

Cheryl stayed pressed against the wall. She kept her eyes closed, but she could feel the elevator approaching. All she wanted to do was escape.

There is a story, she wanted to say. A badly written fairy tale. The story of a woman who'd loved her family and who believed in promises. Empty promises.

Down the hall and around the corner in a conference room, her husband was planning his ride to the U.S. Senate. It was an honor. One he couldn't refuse.

Her insides seized again and she held back the tears. How could he lie and tell her he was retiring?

The elevator door slid open and Cheryl's arm was grasped gently. Her eyes flew open.

"Come on. Get in."

"Chad?" Relief and apprehension warred. "What are you doing here?"

"Offering aid to a friend." He pressed the button for the fifth floor and as the doors slid closed, Cheryl saw Nick running toward her. She shook her head and he stopped.

Right now she couldn't talk to a Crawford. The true depth of her disappointment in her husband and her marriage would burst out, and she wasn't sure she was ready to show that side of her marriage to anyone. She had to face the truth first.

Cheryl kept her back to Chad, and when they exited the elevator she moved under power she didn't know she possessed. He opened his door and Cheryl went inside the single king-size room.

Compared to her suite, this room was a closet. Compared to her husband, Chad was a knight. She was glad for his presence.

Glad he offered her an escape route when she needed one most. "Thank you." A lone tear ran down her face so quickly she didn't have time to stop it. "My God, I'm crying."

Chad moved around her closely. "That's not crying," he said in her ear. "Stop holding everything inside. Nobody is here but you and me. You can scream at the world and it will never leave this room. Cry, Cheryl."

"Why are you pressuring me? Why does everyone want me to do something I don't want to do?"

Her back seized and she arched, waiting for the awful pain to pass. "I haven't cried in five years."

Cheryl walked away from the silent man, her hands shaking and her chest heaving. The sob she tried to contain caught in her throat and she opened her mouth to breathe it out. Only another breath rushed from her lungs and she realized there was no escaping.

She hurried to the door, gripped the knob, and Chad laid a gentle hand on her shoulder. Her head dropped forward and she gulped to hold in her tears. The tremulous gasp moved through her body, and the impulse became stronger than she could resist.

She walked past Chad, sat on the foot of his bed, picked up the cloth beside her, and wept.

Fifteen

"Mom!"

"Cheryl?"

Jett pushed past his father into the suite, the party decorations executed to perfection. Cheryl had even had a mammoth cake made for his father's retirement. The one he and Aunt Keisha ordered seemed small beside the bigger one.

Best Wishes Teaching in South Africa.

Jett spun the cake around and lined it up with the edge of the table. His mother didn't even eat cake anymore. But he bet his father didn't know that. His father didn't know much lately.

Jett faced Justin, hating the look he'd seen on his mother's face, hating his father for putting it there. He'd been silent for too long. "You forced her to leave."

"I didn't mean to, Jett."

"You don't care how she feels, how I feel. You only care about yourself."

"That's not true, son."

He pointed to the cake for his mother. "The teaching offer she's been waiting on for two years comes through, and now you're running for the Senate. I guess she's supposed to go to

Africa alone? Like you've done for every job you've had for the past what, twenty years, all by yourself?"

His father looked around as if those thoughts had never occurred to him. "I didn't want her to go alone. I wanted . . . " He stopped, at a loss.

"You don't want her to go."

"Jett, you don't understand. I've always wanted to be a senator. Ever since I was very young. Almost all of my life has been devoted to public service. I know it might not be fair, but I can't quit and do nothing for two years."

"You can't be her, right?" Jett picked up the special cake his mother had had made for his father's retirement and dropped it into the garbage can. The anger he felt toward his father was so visceral that Jett wanted to hit him.

Once upon a time, he'd thought that his father was this cool guy, with a cool job and high-profile, cool friends. He realized now that his dad was selfish and pathetic.

"Thing is, Dad, you're not even smart enough to know that all she does is work to make you look good and make your life easier. I know worrying would never occur to you, so don't. I'm going with her."

"Your mother and I have problems, but they don't involve you."

"There you go again, Dad, thinking of yourself. My mother's unhappiness affects everything I do. My mother deserves to pursue her dreams and if they take her to Africa or Asia or around the world, I don't care, I'll be by her side."

"Your mother would want you to stay at Tech and graduate."

Now he had some answers? Jett couldn't stay in the room another minute. He brushed past his father.

"Where are you going?"

"To find your wife. What about you, Dad?"

Jett opened the door and Kathy was on the other side, her smoky green eyes full of concern. "Is everything all right?"

"No," he said, as he bent to kiss her. He took the handles of her wheelchair and began to push.

"What can I do to help?"

"Help me find my mother."

Sixteen

Cheryl stood in Chad's bathroom, inspecting her eyes, puffed up and red with no makeup. She looked a mess. She had to face the family and tell them the truth.

She left the bathroom and Chad surged to his feet, his khakis and blue cotton shirt unwrinkled, whereas she felt as if she'd been put through the wringer.

He walked over and eased her slowly into his arms. At first she didn't return his comfort, but the weight of being strong alone was too much. And she wanted to let herself feel.

Being against him was different. He wasn't as broad as Justin, but he wasn't scrawny either. She felt safe here.

Chad didn't pressure her. Didn't try to take her moment of weakness to any level. But her brain kept returning to the fact that Justin was the man her heart had been pledged to. He didn't deserve her though. And the part of her soul that was responsible for protection slid markers into the plus column for Chad.

Cheryl eased back, yet Chad didn't fully release her.

Their cheeks separated and as easy as breathing, he kissed her. And Cheryl kissed him back.

The sparkle of newness brushed at the debris of her marriage and she kept her eyes closed.

When she opened them, a gentle smile curved his lips.

"What are we doing?" she asked as his hands slid down her arms.

"Exploring the infinite possibilities."

"I can't," she said.

"We already have."

He walked her to the door. "My number is stored on your PDA as Mrs. Brown. Call when or if you need me."

He was so young and sure of himself. "Do you mean if?" she asked.

He kissed her again, this time deepening it, then he let her go.

Cheryl accepted the withdrawal of his affection. "This can't happen again. My life is a mess. I'm moving to Africa and I'm married to Justin."

"You just need to know he isn't the only game in town, and if he doesn't get his act together he'll wake up and find another man with his woman. Do what you have to, but I'm here for now."

"I have to go." She turned the doorknob. "Thank you."

"I'm not checking out until noon tomorrow."

Tears rushed to her eyes but didn't fall. "Bye, Chad."

Cheryl took the elevator up and was delivered to the nineteenth floor too quickly. Exiting, she saw Nick first, hands behind his back, walking in a slow circle. He was worried, even if his expression didn't say so.

"There's nothing between Chad and me."

"Not if he could help it."

Nick never minced words. Cheryl loved that about him.

"Not that Justin deserves my loyalty," she said, bringing to the forefront why they were in the hallway now.

"He might have been an ambassador, but nobody ever said he was smart."

Cheryl went into Nick's open arms, the urge to cry continuing to build.

"What are you going to do?" he asked.

"I'm afraid I'm losing him. He wants everything but me. I don't know," she finally answered. "I'm taking the job in South Africa."

Nick smoothed her hair back, the tough marine on hold. His eyes were gentle and held a hint of sadness. "He's a fool, but we've all been there. If you're patient, he'll come around."

She stepped from his embrace and saw the other four Crawford men and their wives. "I don't think we'll have enough time for that," she said before the others engulfed her.

Cheryl didn't have to speak as she was given silent hugs by all of her brothers- and sisters-in-law. Even Mom and Pop Crawford stepped out of the suite and hugged her. "We're praying for you all," Pop told her.

"Thank you." Cheryl took a deep breath. "Where are my parents?"

"Your father wasn't feeling well," Lauren said. "He and your mom went back to their room."

"They were supposed to be staying with me at the house."

"Apparently Justin got them a room here. They've been in Atlanta since yesterday. Your mom wants you to call her when you can."

Was there no end to what he'd do to get his way? Cheryl bet Justin wouldn't have put a thousand dollars on her walking out of that press conference. That was so out of her character.

Well, she wasn't living for him anymore. "Where's Justin?"

"Inside," Julian said, looking pained. Keisha stayed close to his side as they gathered her in a group hug. The tears fell then, and Cheryl wasn't sure what all this sadness meant.

"Call us tomorrow," Julian said. "Congratulations, darlin'."

"Thank you," she said, wiping her eyes.

A chorus of congratulations rained upon her and Cheryl felt bittersweet joy. She'd hoped this would be a joyous moment, but it was what it was.

"Mom. There you are." Jett came down the hall, pushing Kathy at full speed. Everyone parted to let the couple through. Cheryl had to smile.

"Jett, slow down. You're going to give Kathy motion sickness."

"Thank you, Mrs. Crawford. I do feel a little green around the gills." The brown-skinned former catalogue model looked up at Jett with adoration in her eyes. A freak bathroom accident had landed her in the wheelchair, but that hadn't stopped Jett from pursuing her. They'd been together almost a year.

"Sorry, babe. Mom, have you talked to him?"

"I'm going to now. But"—she looked at all of her brothers- and sisters-in-law who seemed ready to hold down the post outside the suite door— "y'all go on home. We'll work this thing out." Cheryl realized she'd taken on the role of carpenter again. She couldn't fix their problems alone. "I don't know what's going to happen, but I'll call. Whatever the outcome. Lauren, will you call my mom and dad and tell them I'll call them at home tomorrow in Columbus?"

"I sure will. Call if you need us," Lauren said, and started down the hall.

"Mom, I'm staying," Jett said, standing every inch of his six-foot-one height.

"I need to speak to your father privately. Take Kathy back to the house and get something to eat. I'll be home shortly."

"Mom—"

"Julian, Nick, Edwin, Michael, Eric," she said softly, the way she used to when he'd act up. Just the threat of his uncles coming over to talk to him had been enough for him to change his behavior. To her relief, Jett backed down.

"Fine. Thirty minutes," he warned, and she knew he meant business. "If I don't hear from you, I'll be back."

Cheryl was sure of Jett's love. Her family's devotion. But she wasn't sure of what was on the other side of the door.

When the elevator door closed, Cheryl walked into the suite and met her husband face-to-face.

"What did you think you were doing?" Justin asked.

"What I should have done when I realized you weren't a man of your word. I should have left you a long time ago."

She walked into the bedroom and to the closet. She had only brought a few items, but she carefully folded them into her garment bag.

"All for a teaching job? I can get you a teaching job right here in Atlanta, Cheryl."

"It's more than just a teaching job." Insulted, she glared at him. "They asked me, not someone else, *me*. And I'm going to take them up on their offer."

"Without consulting me?"

"What?" She couldn't believe that after what he'd put her through this was being made to be her fault.

"You seem to want to make the major decisions in our family now. You wanted me to walk away from a lucrative and important job, Cheryl, just because it fell within your time frame. You didn't care what deals I had going, or that I cared about the job and the people I'd pledged my support to."

She finished with the clothes and moved into the bathroom and came out with her toiletries, which she threw into the suitcase compartments.

"Asking you to leave immediately might not have been fair, but if there's a fair meter, you certainly don't register on it. I'm barely worth your attention anymore unless your life is inconvenienced. You decided to run for the Senate against my wishes. Now, that's unfair."

She slipped out of her dress and into comfortable clothes.

"You're being overly dramatic."

His criticism hurt as much as his breach of trust. Twenty years of marriage boiled down to Justin not getting his way.

"How much is this costing us, Justin?"

"Cheryl, the money belongs to both of us."

"How much?"

"One million dollars."

She staggered a bit as pain tore across her face. "And what if you don't win?"

"I plan on winning, Cheryl."

She walked around him and dragged the bag off the bed.

"You're being unreasonable. I can't go to Africa."

"Then there's nothing more to talk about. If you want to be a senator, live your dream, Justin. But don't expect me to go along with you."

Justin's expression said he couldn't believe she was walking away from him. "Cheryl, can we stop this for one minute? I've always wanted to be a senator. Maybe even president of the United States. Don't you think that's important?"

Fire consumed her dreams of their living happily ever after. "If you knew me, you'd know the answer to that question was no. But this is your road. Take it wherever it leads you."

"Have I not taken care of you? Been there for you?"

Tears flowed down her face. He looked so scared. "If you're not there when I board that plane, I'll—"

"What, Cheryl?" he asked, sarcastically. "You'll leave me?"

"No. You will have already left me."

Seventeen

Cheryl passed Shaw on the way out. Justin noticed that she didn't even bother to speak. They were working opposite sides of the same fence.

Justin thought his head would explode.

Shaw came into the room talking. "We got some preliminary feedback from the press conference. Our numbers—"

"Not now, Shaw."

"Now," she said firmly. "Your life isn't going to get easier. If you can't focus now, we can fire each other and go our separate ways. Or, we'll sit down in this strategy meeting, eat some of this good food—" She eyed the table. "Too bad about the cake. Now let's recap."

Justin grit his teeth.

"The initial response is good from the hotline number we ran at the bottom of each telecast of the press conference."

He mentally tabbed through the agenda from their earlier meeting and a hotline hadn't been discussed. "We have a hotline?"

"The perks of doing business with me," she said, not at all modest. "You lied to me."

"What?" Justin wished he could take back the

evening and start over. He'd have told Cheryl last night, but he'd made love to her, hoping to rid himself of his guilt over his impending decision.

But Shaw? He didn't owe her an explanation about his private life. "Come again?" he asked her.

"Your wife had no idea you were announcing your run for the Senate. Crappy way to treat her, but that's your business. My job is to do damage control."

Justin sat down. "My wife and I had a minor difference of opinion about me running for the Senate. We're working on it, so let's move on."

Shaw regarded him after she'd filled her plate with vegetables. "We have a problem and she just walked out of that door. Either she's on board, or we announce a separation right now before any more damage is done."

"A separation?" he asked, incredulous.

"That's what her leaving constitutes. And, with your approval, that's the way it's going to read in the morning paper."

She gave him a mock newspaper that looked authentic. Justin read the article with his and Cheryl's names placed in the appropriate boxes, and grew nauseated. "You're crazy. Get rid of this."

"What are you going to tell the press?"

"To mind their business. My wife is angry at me for not being straight with her, but we'll get through this. Destroy that story. I don't want anyone to see those lies."

Shaw tossed the article onto the table and finished the last carrot on her plate. "Where does she want to teach?"

"University of South Africa."

"That might not be so bad. Hmm—"

A knock sounded at the door and Justin thought it might be one of his brothers. He was disappointed yet relieved that it was a waiter.

"I was told to collect some of the dishes."

"Come in," Justin said. The waiter began stacking the wrapped plates of vegetables, fruits, and cheeses on the tray. "Nobody was hungry?" he asked.

"Not tonight," Shaw said.

"Hey, aren't you Justin Crawford, the guy who just announced that he was running for the Senate?"

Justin paced the room like a caged animal. He thought he recognized the waiter, but he couldn't really tell. "That's me," he finally answered at Shaw's urging. "What did you say your name was?"

The waiter slipped his hand into his pocket, appearing modest. "Llasllet," he said, without blinking.

"Unusual." Justin frowned when he realized that he sounded like a jerk. Cheryl was better at this than he was. She found just the right platitudes for every situation and was sincere when she said them.

"That's what happens when your mother uses cocaine as a food group."

Justin centered his gaze on the twinkling skyline, speechless. What could he say to that? "You've got a job. You're heading in the right direction."

He heard his own voice, but wouldn't allow his brain to register that he'd said something even more stupid. He mentally zipped his mouth closed and went out onto the windy balcony.

"Thanks. I'll be out of your way in just a minute, sir."

Justin looked down onto the street and wished he were twenty feet below, in his car, driving home to his wife who'd be waiting and willing to help him destress after a hard day.

His shoulders tightened. Right now he had no idea where Cheryl was. Or if they'd ever be the same.

He wanted to go after her right now, but Shaw was still here, and so was the waiter with the ridiculous name.

Justin came back into the room. Llasllet cleared his throat and accepted Justin's twenty-dollar bill without hesitating.

Half the food had been put onto the serving cart, while other trays hadn't been moved.

"Seemed a waste to take it all back. You paid for it."

"Thanks."

Shaw had taken up a post in the far corner with her cell phone, planning, Justin realized. He got close enough to hear something about a debate before she made an eating motion and pointed to him.

Llasllet steered the cart out of the room, and as soon as the door snapped closed Justin consulted his PDA and checked his to-do list.

He didn't know how Shaw had done it, but somehow in the midst of her conversation she'd e-mailed him a message to eat.

His stomach growled for attention, but Justin

was too anxious. Not knowing where Cheryl was had him unusually distracted. His initial high from the press conference was gone, along with a fragment of his pride. He'd thought that somewhere inside Cheryl she would be happy for him and join the team.

This time his gamble hadn't paid off. That was twice, and Justin didn't know if he could make another wager where Cheryl was concerned.

The reporters had sensed there was a story with fresh blood, but only because of Lauren's notoriety and Lea's presence had he been able to selectively answer questions about his decision to run.

Justin glanced around the finely decorated room; Cheryl's touch was everywhere. From the cake to the decorations that swayed in the corners, to the old-fashioned streamers looped around the room. It all looked foolish and fun, but made him feel worse, especially since he had no one to share this moment with.

Justin pulled down the decorations and rolled the banner into the tube he found in the coat closet.

With everything gone, he felt slightly better. His stomach rallied for support and he got a plate of food and sat down, reached for the fake paper, but it was gone.

The plate fell to his feet as he raced for the hallway door. What if Llasllet hadn't been a real waiter?

"Shaw, get off the phone! The newspaper's gone!"

Eighteen

Llasllet? What kind of name was that?

My mother used cocaine as a food group. He'd read that line before. As a headline on a rag newspaper!

He ran down the hall, checking doorways on his way to the elevator. He stabbed the button.

Shaw ran up behind him, her eyes the size of saucers. "I threw the newspaper away."

"No, you didn't. You set it on the table, in plain view for my wife or anyone to see."

"I didn't know it was going to be stolen!"

"The first lesson in politics is never do anything you don't want the world to know about. You should have known better," he said, confronting her.

"It wasn't intentional," Shaw barked.

"I've got to find him," Justin said, as the elevator opened. "Damn, damn, damn."

The serving cart Llasllet had used was the only thing in the empty elevator car.

Justin dug through the plates, hoping the waiter was just a guy who didn't know what he had in his possession. He touched soggy paper and pulled the dripping card from beneath a sweating bowl of ice. Precise printing spelled out *Llasllet,* on the front side with an arrow.

Justin flipped the card over.

Tells All.

The truth hit him like a pallet of bricks. Llasllet was the man's moniker. Tells All was Llasllet backward.

The rag reporter that had been growing in popularity because of his unique disguises had gotten him good. He'd come for a story and had gotten a scoop.

Shaw kept her hand over her mouth. "You should fire me."

"You're right. But you're going to make damned sure that I get elected first."

Justin rushed back to the room, dialed the front desk, and spoke to security. Then he dialed again.

"Julian, meet me at Mom and Dad's in an hour."

His brother chuckled. "No way, man. Are you kidding?"

"What?"

"You obviously don't know what you put the family through today."

"I didn't plan for things to go that way."

"It doesn't sound like you planned anything. You did Cheryl wrong."

"You're supposed to be on my side."

"Even when you dis my favorite sister-in-law? She's family, Justin. Regardless of the fact that she's your wife and the mother of your son, she's our sister and she didn't do anything to us. Get over yourself, candidate. I'll see you tomorrow."

"It'll only look worse in the light of day."

"Bro, you're screwing up," Julian said, patiently. "I feel like I'm talking to one of the kids. Tomorrow, Justin. At the big house. Get some rest."

The weight on Justin's shoulders shifted, making it easier to bear. Tomorrow was just a few hours away. "Yeah. Later."

Shaw listened in on his conversation. Suddenly her eyes brightened, and she dialed her cell phone.

Justin tried Cheryl's cell phone, but she wasn't picking up. When he was done, Shaw ended her call too.

"What was that all about?" she asked.

"Damage control, as you put it. I need to announce my platform tomorrow."

"You're not ready."

"In light of the circumstances, I think I'd better have something important to say sooner than later," he said. "So either you're going to do your job or we can call it an experience and be done with it."

She didn't blink. "I'll put together a press release stating the article was a fraud. But you're going to need Mrs. Crawford to make appearances with you this week. And she's going to have to campaign to show everyone that everything is wonderful. If you can pull that off, you'll be able to lessen the intensity of what's to come."

"I'll do my best." Still unsure about Cheryl, Justin prayed she'd pick up her cell phone. He dialed again and it rang and didn't roll to voice mail.

Was she out with Chad?

Can you blame her? His alter ego snickered.
You're a lying . . . politician.

The false article would only blow a bigger hole
in whatever trust Cheryl might have had in him.
What was he going to do? His wife looked as if
she wasn't coming back. But that couldn't be.
They'd always been together.

Shaw watched him. "You have to make a decision," she said.

"About what?"

"Go with me here for a moment. Announce
your separation. If you deny the article and she
doesn't campaign, then you're going to be per-
ceived as having an unhappy home. Therefore
you can't be a good leader. If you announce your
separation before the article hits the papers, then
you've scooped the scooper. Think about it,"
Shaw said, "and I'll be right back." She went to
the rest room and shut the door.

Justin closed his eyes, and saw snapshots of his
family's life. Cheryl had always been there.
Through every trial and every success. He loved
her, but could he walk away? She wanted him to
give up everything to follow her to Africa. What
did people do all day? He'd been to the continent,
but never for any extended period of time.

Being away for two years could be career sui-
cide. And if he left now, he'd lose every dime he
was about to invest in running for the Senate. A
hefty one million dollars.

That was too risky. He'd started rowing this
boat, now he had to get to the other side.

He and Cheryl would have to work things out.
But what if she wouldn't? She'd threatened him

before. Maybe this was another ultimatum. He knew the phrase was redundant, but maybe she was gambling that he'd give in.

We could separate, he thought, but he couldn't manage to get the words out of his mouth.

They could separate just for the public, and then when Cheryl was done in Africa they could resume their lives.

"I'm sorry." Shaw had reentered the room and thought him asleep. "Let's put the last suggestion on hold and revisit it in the next couple of days. After all, we don't know what he's going to do with that article. I've checked with my sources and nobody has commissioned the article that we know of."

"How accurate are your sources?"

"The absolute top of every major newspaper in the country."

Justin nodded. He didn't know whether to be impressed or worried that she had something to do with this entire setup. Shaw sounded like she cared. He didn't know her well enough to be able to decipher if she was lying.

"Let's develop your campaign platform, Senator."

Justin brought his tired body forward.

"Dean John Stevens has announced his intention to run for the same seat," Shaw told him. She passed him the man's political agenda. "He's known to favor corporate rights, he wants to hold the EPA standards to favor the automakers and cut the police force by twenty percent in favor of private duty enforcement groups and automation. His platform of less government is ridiculous. We can show communities with no police forces and how crime has increased. We can challenge Stevens to live in those communities."

Justin agreed. "But he's also known for private school vouchers, integration, and a one-man, one-vote electoral process. I'm for educating the young and old, but selective equality *is* a misnomer. No such animal exists. The system must be fair in how it rewards, punishes, and protects its citizens. I believe in women's rights, gay rights, the right to bear arms, and a right to privacy, and those are what come to mind off the top of my head. We registered fifteen thousand young adults and five thousand seniors. They want a changing of the guard. That's me."

"Let me ask you something." Shaw stroked a carrot as if it were a cigarette. He wondered how long it'd been since she quit. "How good is your relationship with your son?"

"Tenuous," he said, without further comment.

"That one factor could cost you the election. You registered fifteen thousand students, but after they hear that a cool, drug-free college student whose girlfriend is in a wheelchair is voting for someone else—" She wagged her finger. "They'll run to the other side, just so *you* won't get elected. It's happened before."

Her tactlessness was effective. Justin believed her.

"Let's review the typical publicity strategy and then customize it. In the next twenty-four hours I'll need head shots of your son and wife."

"No problem, but we have to get the word out there to circumvent the article."

"Done. You're going to be on *Larry King Live.*"

"When?" he asked, shocked.

"A week from today."

A knock made Justin and Shaw head for the door. The head of security stood outside. "We couldn't find anyone fitting your guy's description, but we did find these in the loading dock."

Justin took the clothes and shook the man's hand. "Thank you, Officer."

"One more thing. He used the free phone in the lobby. I can have the last call traced, but if this is a criminal matter I will have to write that up in my incident report. I'll have that for your review and signature within the hour."

"This isn't a criminal matter," Justin said.

The man slid a bit closer, his demeanor still serious. "If you have a need for personal security, let me know."

"Thank you for all your help," Shaw said and closed the door. She waited until they were back in the living room of the suite. "I hope you weren't getting ready to hire him. The whole thing could have been an inside job."

"Give me some credit." Justin's cell phone rang and he hurriedly picked it up. "Hello?"

"It's me, Maura. You need to get back here. The final meeting is Tuesday."

For the first time that night, Justin felt real relief. "Where's Herb?"

"Scared he's being replaced."

"Where'd he get that idea?"

"Could be from the announcement that you were resigning."

"Right," he said, duly chastised. "I'll speak to him personally today."

"You fired Chad?" she asked factually.

Justin grimaced. "He fired himself when he thought he was in love with my wife. Did he come back there?"

"No, I think he's still in Atlanta. Boss, the final meeting is day after tomorrow. I'll fax over what you need to be prepared for. After your meeting, we can start packing the essentials so we can all move back home."

"So you're coming home too?"

"Yes."

"I heard through the grapevine that you were involved with someone over there."

"Chad has a big mouth. My friend here isn't ready to take things to the next level, so I'm not waiting for him to get his emotional act together. I'm returning to Atlanta. Mr. Crawford, am I fired?"

That was a question he hadn't expected. "No, not unless you want to pursue other employment."

"I'm not interested in working for anyone else. Will I have the same position?"

"Administrative assistant."

"With a raise?" she bargained.

"You sure do want a lot."

"Twenty percent is good for me," she said, hopeful.

Justin kept quiet, a smile on his face. He knew Maura, and she knew she wasn't getting a raise.

"Twenty-five is even better, thank you."

He couldn't help but laugh. "Fifteen and that's my final offer," he said, surprising himself.

"Deal. What about Herb?" she asked.

"I'll determine what he wants to do when I speak with him. I'll be back in two days."

"Sounds good. See you, boss."

Justin hung up and dialed his second assistant. He couldn't swear to it, but he got the feeling that Maura hadn't been too far away from Herb.

Herb negotiated as well as Maura, but didn't get nearly as much. When faced with Justin's silence, he backed down and settled for five percent.

"Excuse me, but did you just hire your former assistant to work on this campaign?"

"Yes, why?"

"Who is she?"

"Her name is Maura Grider and she's been my AA for five years. My second assistant, Herb, will be joining us as well. It's about time I got my office set up."

"In the future, please clear any personnel additions through me. I'd like to have background checks run on everyone before giving them the green light."

"Maura and Herb are fine employees. They're completely trustworthy."

"Like Chad Brown?"

The flash of anger that hit Justin had been brewing inside for hours. "Who the hell do you think you're talking to?"

"I told you from the beginning I need to lead if you want to win."

"If confronting me every time I make a decision is your version of being a good boss, then you need to work elsewhere."

"Do you want to win, Senator?"

"Do you want to have a job?"

"Touché." Shaw pushed her blond hair over her shoulder. "How about we discuss them and agree."

"And if we don't?"

"You get the first pass and then me. That's my best offer."

Justin considered her for a moment. "I don't like you," he said seriously.

Shaw smiled. "I was just thinking the same about you."

"It this worth it?"

"We have sixty-two days. Do you want to be the next senator of Georgia?"

"Yes."

"Then we should put our personal dislikes aside and figure out a way to circumvent that reporter."

Justin agreed, but wondered if he wasn't making another huge mistake.

Nineteen

"How do the headquarters look?"

Cheryl sat across from Keisha, dining at Justin's. The restaurant wouldn't have been her first choice because the eatery and her husband shared the same name, but the chef had received great reviews, and Cheryl wanted to soak up the Atlanta atmosphere; she'd been away so long.

Keisha gave a noncommittal shrug. "It looks like a typical campaign office. Long on coffee, short on staff."

Cheryl adjusted her Ann Taylor cardigan sweater and tried not to look old in the midst of the young urban professionals.

"How's the studying going?" Keisha asked, then spooned French onion soup into her mouth.

"It's wonderful to learn about the country and the people, but it's overwhelming. I'm humbled by how much I don't know about our people."

"You'll get it, don't worry."

"Hopefully before I'm too old." Cheryl rolled her shoulders and her back cracked. She looked at Keisha and burst out laughing. "My," she complained. "I'm my father."

"Father?" Keisha answered playfully. "I'm Julian."

They laughed again, and the tension that had affected her perception of their relationship these past few weeks eased away. She realized that was what had been bothering her since she'd returned from Ecuador. She and Keisha were closer than sisters, and had been part of the same family for two decades, but somehow negative energy had invaded their space, and Cheryl knew that was her fault.

Keisha gazed at Cheryl with a mixture of sadness and hurt that shone just beneath the surface.

"Are we going to be all right?" Cheryl asked, taking Keisha's hand.

Keisha squeezed. "We're going to be fine."

"What happened?"

"I don't know. I don't want you to go."

Feeling emotional, Cheryl gave them a moment to regain their composure. "I'm not going far. I *have* to go to Africa, Keisha. If I don't, how will I feel about my life when I'm ninety years old? Will I be satisfied that I'd done everything God intended for me? Or did I let someone else dictate my existence?"

"When you put it like that, I agree. I'm being selfish." Keisha pouted. "Who will I talk to?"

"Lauren, Ann, Jade." Cheryl listed their sisters-in-law, wondering how she'd survive without them also. "Terra is coming along nicely."

"They are about the best sisters-in-law a girl could have."

"Hey, don't rule me out," Cheryl scolded. "I'm just a phone call away."

They wiped their damp cheeks. "Tell me the truth, how's my husband doing?" Cheryl asked, finally getting to the reason for the lunch, and her anxiety.

"Not great, but he isn't falling apart. I think he really believes he has a shot. He's got this Web-based initiative that's registered another twenty thousand students. So far, he's been to sixty cities, and people love him. Nobody can ever say Crawfords lack charisma."

"I'm impressed." Cheryl hadn't wanted to be regaled with anecdotes of his success. She wanted to know how he slept at night. If he longed for her. If he'd changed his mind and had chosen her over politics. If he'd been doing badly, even a little, she'd have felt marginally better, but Justin's life seemed just fine. Without her.

"Have the brothers had a family meeting?" Cheryl stared into her Diet Coke, wishing it was rum with Coke over ice.

"Not yet. I think Justin's been avoiding them."

"And they're letting him?"

"Julian mentioned something about letting him hang himself. They're waiting for Justin to come to them. Kind of like they did Nick."

Cheryl understood the thinking, but she wanted her husband back, and if he needed an intervention from his family, she expected them to take care of it.

But maybe that was the problem. She'd always waited for someone else to do things for her. Cheryl chastised herself. Her life was her own. She needed to be more proactive.

"Look, don't bite my head off because I'm just voicing what others have asked me." Keisha sat up straight as if she were conducting an interview.

"What is it?"

"Have you given any thought to teaching . . . locally?"

Cheryl pulled two crisp twenty-dollar bills out of her purse and laid them on the table. "You wouldn't have asked that question of a man. You wouldn't have asked that question of Justin."

"Sweetie—"

"Nobody said a word when Justin took me and Jett with him to Carnesville, Georgia, so he could intern with that crazy black-people-hating clown Jonathan Bugle. We lived in a two-room apartment where the living room and bathroom were separated by a wall no thicker than cardboard. And nobody said a word when the three of us lived in Santiago, Chile. While Justin negotiated better living conditions for missionaries, we didn't have hot running water for sixteen months.

"When we came back home, for months Jett would cling to me each time I would try to put him in the tub. He'd gotten used to being bathed in cold water."

"I'm sorry, I had no idea."

"I don't want you or anyone to think you have to choose sides. I'm going to teach in Africa."

"Even without Justin?"

Cheryl couldn't bring herself to nod that truth into being. She'd slept very little thinking of their lives and what they'd both be walking away from if neither gave in. When she was alone, her insecurities grew. That didn't stop her from believing in a fairy-tale happy ending.

Today she'd been ready to climb the walls wanting to be with him, but Keisha had saved her by being available to have lunch, and Cheryl didn't want to embarrass herself by asking too many questions. She and Justin now lived two floors from each other, but were worlds apart. Nothing Keisha said about Justin would change that reality.

Keisha regarded her across the table. "You sleep in the same bed. Why don't you ask him how he's doing?"

"I moved out," Cheryl said quietly.

"What! Whoa. *Out* out? Did you get an apartment? Come stay with us."

Cheryl grabbed Keisha's hand. "Not out of the house. I moved downstairs to the guest bedroom beside the laundry."

"How long ago?"

Cheryl couldn't meet Keisha's eyes. "Since the evening of the party."

"And you two haven't made up in any manner?"

"No."

Keisha made a punching motion. "Not even for sex?"

"No."

Cheryl and Keisha suppressed identical shudders. Sex wasn't everything, but she still felt the effects of going cold turkey.

Keisha squirmed in her seat. "I'll call the girls. We'll start the boycott tomorrow. That way tonight everyone can get their freak on for the last time for a while."

"Nobody needs to boycott anything. Besides,

you sex fiends won't be able to stick to your word."

"How do you know?" Keisha pressed. "You're doing it."

"I slipped a couple of times," Cheryl confessed.

"This week?"

"No. Two weeks ago when I first came back to Atlanta. Be straight with me, Keisha. Does he miss me?"

Her head bobbed up and down. "Of course he does, darlin'."

Cheryl had been around politicians too long. She could detect a lie a mile away. Justin didn't miss her. He probably never even mentioned her name. The truth stung with the consistency of a swarm of bees.

Maybe the boycott would get his attention, but she doubted it. "Come on," she said. "I've got to hit the books."

Cheryl waved to the waitress, anxious to get outside in the sunlight.

"May I help you?"

She pressed the money into her hand. "Just a five in change for the valet, please."

The woman hesitated, then returned her cash. "Your lunch has been taken care of."

Keisha gave her a bewildered looked.

"By whom?"

"The gentleman in the camel-colored suit and black Kenneth Coles." Her arched eyebrow hiked up and her mouth quirked. "You sure are lucky. Enjoy your day."

Cheryl's gaze snapped to the waitress, who

made it a point of walking back toward their benefactor, her hips working it out in high heels.

Cheryl leaned back in the chair. Her mouth fell open when her gaze landed on Chad.

Twenty

"What are you doing here?"

"Complete coincidence," Chad said smoothly as he grinned down at Cheryl. Tingles raced across her skin.

Even from the other side of the table, Chad smelled great.

Cheryl glanced around, nervous, but no one seemed to be paying them a bit of attention, except Keisha.

"How are you?" He slipped his hand into the pocket of tailored trousers.

"Great. You look great. I'm good," she said, brightly. "Girls' day out. We've been shopping. Couldn't be better."

"Hello," Keisha interrupted. "I'm *Mrs.* Keisha Crawford. And you are?"

Chad turned his charming smile on Keisha. "Embarrassed by my rudeness. I'm Chad Brown. A pleasure to meet you."

"You look familiar. Have we met before?"

"No, ma'am, but I used to work for Justin."

"Used to?" Cheryl said, then bit her tongue. He would quit. Especially now that Justin was running for public office. "Of course." She gestured to the newspaper. "Are you job hunting?"

He looked amused. "Not from the newspaper."

Cheryl sucked in her lips. She didn't realize how unsophisticated she'd sounded until now.

"Thank you for lunch," Keisha told him. "Please, join us?"

"Oh no. Chad probably has something else to do." Cheryl jumped in, knowing she was too nervous, and if her skittishness showed, Keisha would be on to her.

"Don't mind if I do." Chad slipped between the tables and sat next to Cheryl. Having him beside her made her forget what she'd eaten for lunch. With him there, she abandoned thoughts of the future and wanted only to think about now. Lately he'd been the subject of more thoughts than she cared to acknowledge.

Both Chad and Keisha regarded her. He with amusement, Keisha with suspicion. She tried to stop acting as if they had something to hide.

"What's going on between you two?" Keisha demanded.

Cheryl crossed her legs and began to fan herself with Chad's newspaper. "Nothing at all, right, Chad?"

"The truth is that I like Cheryl more than I should. I have a serious jones for her. Unfortunately, she's married to your . . . ?"

"Brother-in-law," Keisha supplied, her questioning gaze flipping between them.

"Another beautiful woman goes to the light-skinned, gray-eyed brothers." He shook his head regretfully. "What's left for the regular guys who put their pants on one leg at a time?"

She smiled at Chad. "You are quite a piece of work. I have a daughter that would be perfect for you. Unless"—she tapped the table in front of Cheryl—"you invited me to lunch to tell me something else."

Cheryl gave her a "get real" look, and re-folded the newspaper. Nervous tension ran through her veins like a narcotic. "I love Justin, and Chad knows that."

"So what's this air between you two? There's energy here like something happened." She gasped. "Did you sleep with him?"

"No!"

Keisha studied them both. "You're playing with fire, do you hear me?"

"Keisha—" Cheryl warned. "Don't get your thoughts moving in the wrong direction. Nothing has happened between us."

"I don't mind fire," he added, gazing at Cheryl intimately. "When it's worth it."

"Chad, be quiet. You're not helping me."

"Because you won't give me a chance," he said, just as quietly.

"This is bad," Keisha predicted, shaking her head. "Does Justin know how you feel about his wife?"

"I doubt it. He'd have me fired a year ago."

"Nothing is going on," Cheryl ground out, wanting to end the conversation. "Now let's move on. What are you doing here, Chad?"

"Blind date. Didn't work out, though. She wasn't tall and brown-skinned, with long hair and a pretty smile. She didn't favor pearls on Wednesdays and she didn't know jack about the electoral process. She didn't even know where Ecuador was. I sent her home in a cab."

Both ladies laughed.

"Wow," Keisha said. "You've got it bad." She picked up the newspaper Cheryl had just dropped. "My sister-in-law is devoted to her husband, so why are you still interested?"

He gazed at Cheryl and she couldn't help but feel wanted. Chad was handsome and harmless because she wouldn't let things go further. But if her heart wasn't otherwise preoccupied, she could imagine the possibilities.

"I have the grass-is-greener syndrome," Chad confessed. "I was in Cheryl detox for two weeks, but today I slipped," he said, winding down his amusing tale.

Cheryl expected Keisha to trade witty repartees, but her slack expression made Cheryl look down. "Keisha, are you all right? What are you reading?"

Growing concerned, she took the newspaper from Keisha's hands and saw the photo. Justin was on one half of the paper smiling, his arm raised in victory. A lightning bolt split the photo and Cheryl had to unfold the paper to see the rest.

Her breath caught in her throat. She was on the other side, looking at the back of his head, fury etched into her unsmiling face.

The caption said it all. CANDIDATE AND WIFE: SEPARATED.

Twenty-one

Daylight issued a final snub at the approaching twilight by flouncing a rainbow of colors on the horizon.

Because of the rain, traffic had come to a standstill on I-85 S, but Cheryl had sat in gridlock and didn't care. She was separated. What did that mean? Was she supposed to move out of the house? Where? She'd never dreamt she and Justin would ever be apart. She drove into the garage and had to make herself go into the house.

There wasn't a protocol for finding out that a husband didn't want to be married anymore, that's why most women didn't see it coming. Cheryl hated that she'd joined their ranks.

She wanted to rage at the world, but mostly she wanted to beat the hell out of Justin.

Once she admitted to that very human urge to hurt him as much as he'd hurt her, she felt the internal shift to full-fledged anguish.

Why had Justin done this? He'd had ample opportunities to tell her they were over. After all, they still shared a house.

But he obviously had no respect for her. Or

else he wouldn't have pulled this stupid Hollywood stunt.

Her cell phone rang. Keisha again.

"Hey." Cheryl dropped her bag and keys on the granite countertop.

"Sweetie, I wish you'd let me come over."

"No. I'm numb," she said honestly.

Cheryl didn't think she could endure any more crying. Keisha had fallen apart at the table in Justin's.

Cheryl had wanted to cry too, but hadn't. She'd been in pain so long that the final blow was almost a relief.

She hadn't known how to function in the role of comforter, especially since she was the victim, but the impact on the entire family had been overwhelming.

Everybody had read the article and all the lies, and had started calling as she drove home.

She could feel their pain over the phone, hear the anger in the voices of her brothers-in-law, and when Ma and Pop Crawford had called, Cheryl had been tempted not to answer.

Their questions had been the same: Where was Justin? Why had this happened? Was there anything they could do?

And her answer each time had been *I don't know.*

Cheryl was glad that she'd insisted that Chad drive Keisha home. She knew the Crawfords too well. According to Chad, there'd been ten of them waiting when the car pulled up. Cheryl knew that they would have sucked her into the fold, until Justin came to his senses.

But Cheryl didn't want love built on threats, duress, or guilt. Once upon a time she and Justin had loved each other unconditionally. If they couldn't find that pure love that had brought them together, she wouldn't have any love at all. Not from Justin.

"Keisha, stay home. I've got to face Justin alone."

"Did he get in yet?" The defensive tone in Keisha's voice provided an anchor for Cheryl.

"No. But that will give me time to get my things together and go to Mom and Dad's for a couple of days. They will probably appreciate a visit from their daughter."

"You don't have to go alone. Let me or one of the girls take you. Lauren's not doing anything right now."

Cheryl smiled at how easily Keisha volunteered the other women in the family. Keisha may have married into the Crawfords, but their mentality ran in her blood.

Cheryl didn't need to be watched. She wasn't going to fall apart. The self-pity she felt clawing for a piece of her heart would eventually find a stabilizer. Then she'd deal with the useless emotion and be done with it. Right now she had to start thinking about her life without her husband.

"Look, Keisha," she said, "I'm already tired. If I'm too worn out after I pack, I'll stay overnight with you guys and drive to Columbus in the morning."

"Perfect." Keisha exhaled, sounding relieved. "Call me before you head over."

"I will."

Cheryl asked for forgiveness for lying to the woman that was like her big sister. She had no intention of spending the night. She wanted to be alone. She'd just spent two decades with Justin. She didn't want to reduce her marriage to snippets of hateful words she wouldn't be able to take back. She was leaving, but she didn't want a Crawford to save her.

As she recalled his behavior this last couple months, she began packing. The faster her suitcases filled, the sadder she became. She didn't want to be home when he got there.

Maybe she'd return to Ecuador.

Since Justin was no longer an ambassador, Cheryl wasn't sure if they still had travel benefits, but when she got the answers she felt a sense of accomplishment.

She had grabbed the phone book and started dialing the airlines when her cell phone rang. "Mrs. Brown?" A shiver of nervousness rushed through her. "Cheryl Crawford," she answered.

"Hey." Chad's voice faded, sounding grave. "How are you holding up?"

"I'm okay. Packing."

"Where are you going?"

"A hotel for the night. Then back to Ecuador."

"That's a coincidence. I just made my reservations to return for my things."

"When are you leaving?"

"Tomorrow afternoon."

Cheryl didn't want to travel alone. Didn't want to have all that downtime to think about what had gone wrong with her marriage. She wanted to talk about something other than herself. And when avoiding her pain got to be too much for her small shoulders to bear, she wanted to be with a friend whose life didn't revolve around the Crawfords. And didn't revolve around her.

"If it's not an imposition, I'd like to . . ."

"What can I do for you?" It wasn't his words that took her on a journey, but the tone of his voice. The soft bass rocked her in the cradle of a newness that was so refreshing she was almost knee deep before she yanked her leg out of his hypnotic quicksand.

Chad didn't know what a temptation he presented. At the moment, her heart ached so bad that it would be easy to leap from the shallow into the deep end of the pool of life. And with two competitive, aggressive men vying for her attention, someone would drown. She had to keep Chad under control. Otherwise things would get too messy.

"Chad, do you think I could make my reservations for the same flight as yours? Maybe we can share a car back to the house."

"Is that all we can share?"

"Don't pressure me," she snapped. She lowered her voice but didn't apologize. "I'm trying to move forward," she said, knowing he wanted her in his lane. A part of her was curious enough to look, not yet brave enough to venture in. "Give me some time."

The silence between them lengthened. Cheryl almost preferred he be vocal like the Crawfords. But that wasn't his style.

"I'll make the reservations," he said gently, feeling her angst and moving away from it. "By the way, I got a message from Justin."

"What did he say?"

"That he knows I'm in love with you, and if I know what's good for me I'll leave you alone. Then he fired me."

Her breath came in sharply. "You can't possibly love me."

"Don't tell me how I feel."

His voice wasn't hard but sure, and her marriage *was* falling apart. Although the man she loved was emotionally out of tune, her heart still chimed for him.

"Chad, I don't know how I feel about you. I want to be your friend right now because I don't have any I'm not related to. I still love my husband, but he doesn't love me the same way. So I'm scared. I can't kiss you, Chad, without feeling intense guilt. I'm Justin's wife. I don't want to destroy something that was once"—her voice dropped—"and still is sacred to me."

"I can't be your friend," he said matter-of-factly. "I'm in love with you. I would lie, but I thought you were over liars. So maybe we can settle on just being cool. Until . . . we decide otherwise."

The ball of tension in her chest lessened under a long sigh. "I hear you," she said softly. "We're cool."

"Your reservations will be made for tomorrow, so be at the airport at four o'clock tomorrow afternoon. Cheryl?"

"Yes," she said, grateful that he would take care of the arrangements.

"You're a smart, sexy-as-hell teacher who

earned a job teaching in Africa because of merit, not contacts. Never forget how special you are. Good night, lady," he said and hung up.

Tears built in her eyes, but Cheryl squeezed hard, counting to three before they went away. There was no time for tears. She still had to finish packing and find a hotel room. If she could help it, she wouldn't be in the house when Justin got home.

Two hours later, her suitcases were sitting by the garage door and her back was singing a pitiful tune. She had one more decision to make for the night and she dialed directory assistance. "The Marriott, no, Hotel Sofitel." *No*, she thought. She'd have to get on 285 then off at Lenox Road.

"Just a moment, please," the automated voice said.

While she waited, Cheryl remembered the hotel's insignia, and when the operator answered she got the information, called, and made a reservation for one week. In a week, she reasoned, she'd know the next direction for her life.

She lugged the suitcases to the car and was back in the house when Justin's garage door started to go up.

Panic hit her front and center. What would he say when he saw her there? Would he demand she leave?

The Christmas present Lauren had given her caught her eye, but Cheryl left the porcelain Lladro angel in the glass-enclosed display case.

This house was hers, too. She wasn't going to steal from herself.

Justin headed for her room, his voice bouncing off the hallway walls. She opened the door. "You looking for me?"

"Cheryl," he said, sounding relieved. "Where were you? I've been calling your cell phone for hours."

"I've been preparing to leave."

"Why?"

"Justin, don't pretend with me. What you did was wrong. Did your campaign need that much of a boost?"

"I didn't have anything to do with that mistake."

She considered his words for a moment. "Do you think I'm stupid?"

"It was a terrible misunderstanding," he rephrased, his tone making it clear he had dismissed the impact the article would have on her life. Of course he didn't care that she looked like a gold-digging woman out for her husband's legacy.

The steady roll of a drumbeat started in the distance, growing closer.

For a split second, Cheryl thought it could be an approaching tornado, but the loud noise didn't make the whole house tremble. The rumble centered over the roof of their home, crisscrossing spotlights flickering.

A helicopter. "You've got to be kidding." Incredulous, she yanked back the drapes and glared up. Two circled like crow over a meal.

"Forget them, Cheryl. Will you please look at me?"

Cheryl steeled her heart against her husband's

pleas. If she looked at him, she would say all that had been unsaid.

Even as she stood there contemplating how she'd handle him, the truth emerged like a naked toddler after a bath. Justin had been feeding her lies for years. Realizing *their* dream. There was no *their* to him. He had lived the life he wanted, and as long as she'd been willing to go along for the ride, all had been well.

Unknowingly, she'd been in a competition, even in bed. He'd always made her climax first, so that his sense of right remained intact.

In bed, they didn't talk, or laugh, or even read a book together. They had sex. Primal, raw copulating that either could have gotten anywhere. She'd created a false world for them. Cheryl had loved their intimate time together, the space of their mouths being close, their gazes locked as they'd shared a breath, the physical high that accompanied a powerful orgasm, knowing that she'd been the woman that had made it happen for him.

Cheryl stood three feet from her husband and realized that today was the first day she'd ever really known him.

"What will you say that I haven't already heard? You had nothing to do with this? Of course you did. It's ten at night. That article hit the streets in the morning edition. Where the hell have you been?"

His head snapped back at her cursing. *Good*. He ought to be surprised. Life was about to get crazier.

"I've been trying to get the article stopped, and

when I couldn't I had to find a way to circumvent the impact."

Cheryl looked up, the sound of the chopper's blades taking away pieces of her heart. "So you've been working on spinning this. In your favor, Justin? Are you so consumed by thoughts only of you?"

"Of course not. I never wanted to hurt you."

"That's hard to believe with this dagger-size pain in my chest! This is a blessing," Cheryl admitted, swallowing her tears. "I wanted out and now I'm out."

Justin caught her arm and she glared at his fingers. "I've been trying like hell to stop that article. Why won't you believe me?"

"Justin." She stopped speaking and swallowed. "Talk to me, baby."

She yanked her arm away from him. "I'm not your baby! If you can't be honest, then why are you with me?"

"I'm being honest."

"Then who wrote those vile lies? Who hates me so much that they'd try to ruin my life?"

"Shaw wrote the article. She thought that when you walked out of the press conference, you weren't coming back."

"She was right. But how could she make any determination about our lives without your consent? And if she did, tell me she's unemployed."

"Cheryl." His tone was overly patient. "The reporter snuck into the suite and took the article. That wasn't her fault."

"It wasn't mine," Cheryl insisted.

"You're going in the wrong direction." His head fell back, his mouth quirked. "It was a mistake. Can we sit down and talk about this?"

"Talking won't resolve anything. I don't know if I can trust you. I don't want to be lied to."

Her voice cracked and Justin wanted to die. He'd hurt Cheryl in unbelievable ways. She looked as if she was going to cry. Frustration and anger glittered in her eyes.

"I don't like this invasion of my privacy. I hate this disregard for my feelings. I hate it!"

She started out of the kitchen and Justin touched her again. "Okay, Cheryl, please." She pulled away and he released her. "I'll fix this."

Justin opened his phone and hit SEND. A few seconds passed before he spoke. "This is Justin Crawford. There are helicopters hovering over my home and they are frightening my family. This is a residential neighborhood and the airspace is protected. I want the helicopters removed."

He cut the phone off and put it on the table. He hadn't let his wife's hand go, not knowing when he'd touch her again. It seemed as if months had passed since he'd held her. He couldn't go another minute without fulfilling that one wish.

She was still angry with him, the tilt of her jaw said so, but he moved a little closer to test how she'd feel about him entering her personal space. Her wrist went slack and her hand turned into his. Yet her back remained to him.

The whirl of the helicopters faded and they

were cast into blissful silence. His mouth skimmed her neck.

"Fix the rest," she said, her head falling to the side.

He moved his hand up her abdomen and guided her backside into him.

"I'll call a press conference and set the record straight. And then I'll tell them to leave you alone. That you're not part of the campaign and to focus all of their attention on me."

"Do it now."

"Now, sweetheart?" he repeated, surprised at the unfettered demand.

"Yes, now."

Justin wanted Cheryl to turn around and face him, but felt he couldn't make requests until he'd put an end to her anger.

He made a call to Shaw. The press conference would be held in two days. He hoped this would pacify Cheryl and show her that his intentions were not harmful. The stiffness in her shoulders eased a bit. Once upon a time she'd have yielded and come into his arms. They'd have made love to the unspoken apology. Now even as his arousal pressed against her back, she hadn't turned into him.

"Cheryl, I need you." She turned. In her eyes was the beginning glow of forgiveness.

His arousal slackened, to his surprise.

"What is it?"

"Shaw suggested that we be seen together . . . campaigning." Her hands shot off his shoulders. "It would help me a lot," he explained, trying to make her understand.

"Why should I, *again*, Justin? You've made a liar out of me."

"I never meant to. I thought you loved me."

"I do. But it's not the same."

"We're talking, aren't we? I'll make the rest up to you."

The way she looked at him made him think he'd just been in a car wreck. "You can't."

"Cheryl, I don't want a divorce. I don't want to be separated. I want you to be happy and to teach. I want to be senator of Georgia. I want us to both get what we want."

"In the real world, I'm going to Africa, and I want you to come with me. Just like when Jett and I went to Carnesville and Santiago with you."

"That was different."

"Because you perceive that I had nothing to give up? Is that what you're saying?"

"We were a team." His head felt fuzzy from all the arguing. He and Cheryl never argued. They'd always been working for a common goal. His common goal, he realized.

"Not when you don't play fair. I won't refute the newspaper article, because it's true. Good-bye."

"Baby, where are you going?"

As tears streamed down her face, she walked into the kitchen and gathered her purse and keys. "None of your business, considering you're about to become my ex-husband."

Twenty-two

"It's been two weeks. I can't believe you let her go."

After having slept badly the night before, Justin met his brothers at their parent's house the next morning. They sat around the dining room table, and Justin felt as if he were in court, his five brothers his judge and jury.

"I didn't want her to leave," he explained to his bleary-eyed siblings. "I apologized and explained what happened. Her mind was already made up."

"No, it wasn't. She was in a restaurant and saw the article in the paper. When did she have time to make it up? Between the coffee and the check?" Eric asked him.

"I'm just saying when I got home her bags were already in the car."

"That's because she'd just found out—I won't say it again. You're not as stupid as you pretend." Eric threw up his hands.

"Come on!" Justin practically shouted. "We're separated because Cheryl wants us to be. *I* explained. *I* apologized. She didn't want to hear anything I had to say."

Justin's head thudded as he remembered how

he'd felt watching Cheryl walk out. He'd wanted to run after her. Grab her and bring her back into the house. Hold her until she didn't want to leave anymore. But going after her meant he had to give up his dream. No man should ever have to make that choice.

They hadn't shared a bed in weeks, and Justin thought about how close he'd been last night to claiming his wife.

Beyond wanting her physically, he missed her presence in his life. He missed her touch, and the care she took of him. There was no one to share *The New York Times* with, and early this morning he'd found this month's issue of *Black Enterprise* magazine where the housekeeper had put it.

Cheryl usually got to it first and would read him articles while she lounged on the bed. When they were young, they'd devoure the articles on how to build wealth, and in nearly twenty years they'd accumulated enough income to live comfortably for the rest of their lives. But nothing had been the same since they'd left Ecuador.

Things hadn't been good in a long time.

In a moment of weakness somewhere before dawn, he'd called Cheryl's cell phone, but she hadn't answered. She obviously had better things to do than forgive her husband. He wondered if Chad was still in the picture.

Edwin folded his hands on the table. "Why should she come back? What's changed."

"I was hoping she'd changed her mind."

"Why does everyone have to change for you, Justin? I was embarrassed that you made this grand announcement with her begging you not to do it. That was pathetic."

"I—" He stumbled. "I didn't know she'd leave. I thought she'd see how important this was to everyone and come around."

"I knew better than that in the kitchen the day Jada was born," Michael added dryly.

Justin searched around for support. "The environment in Africa is hostile."

"And what's your point?" Julian threw in. "You act as if the entire country is at war, and it isn't. You're generalizing and it's not going to fly. You tried to punk off your wife and she called your bluff."

"As far as I'm concerned, that's all the more reason for you to go. Why can't you just do this for her?" Edwin asked, trying to reason with him. "The assignment is only twenty-four months long. Not the rest of your life."

"I don't want to live in Africa," he finally said.

"Why not?"

"Because . . ."

"Is that all you have to say?" Disgusted, Eric looked like he'd been up all night. "I didn't come here for this. Bottom line, you're selfish. And if this is how you're going to treat your wife, I'm going home to bed and you can continue your little meeting without me."

Justin hadn't ever been out of favor with his brothers before. He had expected their anger, but not their disloyalty.

"You're walking out? You're not the same brother who drank himself stupid for almost a year? The same man who needed his family to support him through his difficulties."

"Yeah, that was me, the dumbest man you've ever seen. Drunk every damn day because my wife had just died in a plane crash. But I didn't treat her like crap in front of the whole family and then expect her to forgive me. I didn't let someone else air her final secrets."

Nick sat forward but didn't speak as Eric continued on his rampage.

"I buried my wife's secrets with her. You know why? Because even though she wasn't the same woman I married, I still loved her and respected her."

"You don't owe him an explanation about a damned thing," Nick cut in, his eyes the color of thunderclouds. "If he wants to act like an idiot and treat his wife like crap, he deserves to get the crap kicked out of him."

The conversation was going places Justin had never trod. He hadn't meant to insult his brother or his dead wife's memory.

"Eric, I'm sorry. I didn't mean anything against you or Marie, God rest her soul, but Cheryl and I are different. I've been in politics for too many years to let my career fall off a cliff because my wife wants to be exotic. You all have the careers you want."

"Somebody, please reason with him," Eric said, stifling a yawn. "He's drunk on delusions of grandeur."

"I know what I want out of life," Justin argued. "I think we'd be having a different conversation if Lauren asked you to move to a foreign country.

I make the money in the family. How are we supposed to live? What would you do, Eric? Any of you?"

A wry smile crinkled Eric's face.

Nick sat back in his chair and his brother Edwin shook his head.

"For the record," Eric replied, "my wife has earned ten times more than me for the past five years. As for moving to a foreign country, I'd do the same things I do now, Einstein. I'd move and I'd work. I'd administer to the sick, and if some miracle occurred and all the sick people in the Philippines or Russia or . . . where were we last year?"

"Africa," Nick supplied.

"Right," he said dryly. "*Africa.* And if somehow they were able to eradicate all diseases while I was there, I'd find a way to bring that knowledge back home."

"I've been in jungles a hundred times longer than you've had this dream," Nick said. "Don't ask us what we'd do. You can't compare your life to mine. We've all been where you are, and if you're not bright enough to listen to us, suffer the consequences."

"I'm sorry you all feel this way," Justin said, disappointed. Even in Nick's darkest hours, Justin had stood by him. Now he was a colonel in the corps and his ego was too big for his shoulders. Ever since Nick had returned three years ago, he'd assumed a role in the family that Justin had always enjoyed. He'd been the go-to guy. Even Cheryl called Nick before asking her own husband. Justin hadn't realized how much it bothered him until now.

"You don't love her anymore," Nick surmised, the judge of this biased jury.

"I love my wife! I've always loved her, but we can get what we need from each other right here in Atlanta. In case you didn't know, advances in medicine in Africa aren't on par with the United States. Many people are sick and dying from HIV and AIDS. Things we take for granted like immunizations and good health care don't exist, not that people don't want them too, but they aren't getting enough international support to help the needy, let alone the healthy.

"Nurses are dying from the diseases they treat, and the world has largely forgotten the country that birthed civilization. If I were in the Senate, I could at least be an advocate for better health care."

"That's all well and good, but that's not why you don't want to go." Michael had been quiet for a while. As the other attorney in the family, he was a born litigator, but since his marriage to Terra he'd been as mellow as fine wine.

He flicked the wheels on one of the kids' Hot Wheel cars as he talked. "I read that same article in the Sunday paper, and I'm sure I'll hear this somewhere along your campaign trail. But don't lie just to pacify us. If you do, then you're just like every other politician who says what he thinks people want to hear so he can get elected. I think you should go to Africa. The bottom line is that if you can do more good here, then you should stay."

"I can't believe this," Julian snapped. "You two don't know what you're saying. Michael, you have no responsibility and little accountability to anyone."

"And that makes what I've said less important?"

"His wife has already left him. Do you have to lose Jett too?" Edwin reasoned.

Justin shook his head. "I can't lose Jett. We'll find a way back. Right now he's too angry."

"And rightfully so," Edwin said, quietly. "He's a man, Justin, and he sees how you're hurting his mother. You'll have to reckon with him before anything else good will happen for you."

"Don't be so ominous. I don't intend to lose my family. Cheryl and I have been heading in this direction for some time now. I've tried to make her happy. She didn't have to take this job in Africa. She can teach here."

"I suppose, in your eminent wisdom, you have the perfect job for her?" Julian asked.

"I'm sure I could find her one."

"You made an agreement that she would work after Jett went to college," Eric said.

"We did, but I didn't know this opportunity would come up."

"I'm sure it was news to her that achieving her goals for her life was contingent upon you not having anything better to do."

"She'll come back," Justin told them, unable to understand their anger.

"You think you're such a catch that Cheryl will wait for you?" Julian asked from the window. "Not only is she an attractive woman, she's a family woman. It won't take someone long to figure that out. Can you handle that, Senator?"

Justin didn't want to admit that those very thoughts had chased him all night. And the idea of losing his wife to a man like Chad Brown made him sick.

"No," Justin admitted honestly. "But I don't know what else to do."

"You've got it backward. It's not job, then family, then God somewhere at the bottom."

"I know, Julian. And I know Cheryl and I can work this out. She just needs time to cool off."

Julian approached the table. "If you're willing to take the chance that the man that's already chasing her won't catch her, you should be able to handle whatever is thrown at you."

"What man?" Eric asked.

"Yeah," Nick said, suddenly amused. "What man is this?"

"That situation is under control." Justin had made a few calls before he came to his parents' house and recommended Chad for the ambassadorship in Ecuador. The approval of the president was necessary, but Justin kept his hopes up that soon Chad would no longer be a distraction in his wife's life.

"Keisha told me all about him. He's younger than you by what, five years? Watch out, Justin. You might not want to go to Africa, but he will."

"He won't be—"

"I need to get going soon," Julian said. "My wife needs me to convince her that not making love isn't going to get you and Cheryl back together."

"What?" Justin demanded. What else was he being blamed for?

One by one his brothers rose, except for Nick.

"You mean the women have been holding out because of him?" Eric asked. "Lauren wouldn't tell me. She just said it was to support the sisterhood, whatever that meant."

Nick started laughing and couldn't stop.

"What the hell is your problem?" Michael demanded.

"I haven't gotten any in weeks. I wondered why you boys all looked worse for the wear." He looked at Justin. "You'd better shape up. Five minutes after my wife's six-week checkup, it's on."

Eric, Michael and Edwin left, leaving Julian and Nick with Justin.

"How much is this campaign costing you?"

"What do you care?" Justin demanded, his head pounding. He still had a full day of campaigning ahead.

"Probably a million or two. Three, maybe," Nick said.

Justin got in Nick's face. "I'm sick of you thinking you can treat me like I'm one of your Marine Corps underlings."

"And I'm sick of you only thinking about yourself."

"What I do with my finances is my business."

"Not when half of the assets belong to your wife," Julian informed him. "This was delivered this morning."

Justin opened the legal document and staggered. He was glad the chair he'd been in for the better part of an hour was still behind him.

Cheryl had filed for a legal separation and had asked for one half of their physical and financial assets. Justin had spent nearly a million on the campaign. That left him four hundred thousand dollars. The other million and a half, Cheryl was asking for.

"Can she do this? I worked all those years."

"Yeah, but she worked to make the money grow in the stock market. She's got a sharp business mind. And according to this document, she's using it."

Nick patted him on the shoulder. "You should probably get home and decide what items you want to negotiate for. The house will probably go to her since you took the cash."

Julian nodded and pursed his lips. "The for-sale sign went up about an hour ago."

"Your childish pranks aren't funny."

"Who's playing?" Julian said coldly. "You're the only one not taking life seriously. I heard talk about a garage sale."

Justin snatched the papers and ran to his car. He had to talk to Cheryl.

Julian watched his brother leave, his tires smoking as he peeled away from the curb.

"Is she really selling?" Nick asked.

"As of right now, she is."

He raised his cell phone to his ear. "Cheryl, it's Julian. If you go by the house, don't be alarmed about the for-sale sign in the front yard. We're having a Crawford intervention. Love you, darlin'. Bye."

"That's cruel," Nick said, and gave Julian a proud pat on the back. "I wish I'd thought of it."

Twenty-three

In the private viewing room on the Georgia State campus, Cheryl's gaze was riveted to the image before her. A lean, short-haired Sowetan woman named Annie graced the screen with a gentle presence.

On this third disc of documentaries, the lives of the women depicted were of little joy. From disease to birth, abuse and death, they'd seen and endured it all.

Cheryl was glad Chad had told her how to rent the private studio. She wasn't going back to his place as he suggested and her hotel room didn't have DVD accommodations for guests, preferring people to rent movies from the TV. Somehow she didn't think this would be on their playlist.

Cheryl knew that, had she watched the documentaries with someone else, she'd have curtailed her emotions. Now that she was on her own, she vowed to stop censoring herself. At times she laughed at some of the stories told by the women, but most of the time she could only rock herself, as she would them if they were near her.

Looking at Annie, Cheryl wondered what her

life had been like before she'd been sold into slavery at eleven by her father.

Annie was fifteen and looked twenty years older, the ravages of eighteen-hour days etched into her smile. Although Annie wouldn't admit to abuse at the hands of her owners, the stripes on her legs and the graying of her right eye told stories her mouth didn't reveal. Cheryl found her remarkable in that she still hoped her family would one day buy her freedom.

Cheryl's cell phone vibrated on the table. The small screen flashed Justin's name. The narrator's voice that had captivated her attention for two hours began to drone.

She had picked up the phone, her thumb hovering over the phone icon, when the vibrating stopped.

She breathed a sigh of relief and then dropped it onto her lap when it vibrated again, startling her. A text message awaited. She read the odd message from Julian, then understood. They were trying to get Justin back for her.

How Crawford of them, she thought, feeling a blend of love and sadness. Her own husband hadn't gone to any lengths to get her back home, so why should she let his brothers deceive him on her behalf?

Because she still loved him and she trusted them. The brothers would handle Justin however they saw fit. She'd have to follow her own mind on this one.

Cheryl returned her attention to the documentary.

Annie wasn't allowed to go outside, except to

do chores. She wasn't allowed to go to the market and had never left the town she'd lived in since she'd been bought.

In her own way, she loved the children she took care of, although they had the power to punish her. Annie's hopeful spirit stirred Cheryl's maternal instincts. She was scribbling notes on a pad for lesson plans when her cell phone vibrated again.

Jumping, she set it on the tabletop. Physically, she ached for Justin in ways that made her blush, and intensified the loneliness. Maybe a reconciliation was in the wind.

She picked up the phone as Annie fell to her knees and started to wail. The awful keening sound echoed like a death knell, and Cheryl's eyes teared. She was wondering what had happened when the narrator continued.

"Annie's father died of AIDS sixteen months after he sold her, her mother, five months later. Annie is devastated to know that no one will ever come for her."

The vibrating continued. "Hello," she said, her throat tight with emotion.

"Cheryl, it's me. How are you? Where are you?"

The sound of Justin's voice made her want to run to him. His voice alone made her want to bury her face in his neck and make love to him until they'd both had enough. But that short-term fix had caused a big divide in their reality. Maybe since some time had passed, they'd really talk and figure out how they were going to resolve their problems.

"I'm fine, Justin. What's going on?"

"You're suing me?"

She dug her heels into the floor. Julian had said something about that in his message.

"Please don't make any more deductions from our bank account," she said.

"You couldn't have just talked to me? We've been able to talk about anything for the past twenty years. And you had to have papers drawn up to tell me not to withdraw any more money? Don't you think that's a little harsh?"

"Not as harsh as finding out that without my knowledge or agreement, you withdrew a million dollars to run for the Senate."

The credits rolled up the screen and Cheryl put her head in her hand. In all of her daydreaming of what their first conversation would be like, she hadn't imagined that they'd be fighting over money. Sure she was mad about it, but that wasn't their biggest problem.

Where was the apology, the repentance, and the forgiveness?

Was the only reason he called that he'd been served?

The papers had been fake, but her feelings weren't.

She bit her lip but not the words. "Do you miss me, Justin?"

"Of course. I want us to be the way we were."

But she hadn't been happy that way. And he knew that.

Cheryl tried to find the good in his words. "You mean from way back in the day. Loving and good to each other. And happy. Do you remember those times?"

"Of course." His voice caressed her intimately. "I miss you. From the bottom of my heart."

"What else is down there?"

"What?" he asked, and she felt a little of the glow fade.

"What will you do to make things better, Justin?"

"I made love to you every night. I made sure every single one of your needs was met. You were never in the dark or hungry or physically abused. I did the best I could for you and Jett. And you let me be ambitious. You helped me thrive. And now I don't know how to be any other way."

The ache inside her grew. "Can I tell you how I feel?"

"Yes, baby."

"Don't—" she started, then stopped. "I hurt for you, Justin. I miss the days of us taking Jett to the park, and I miss our late night talks about our future. Even when we lost our second baby and discovered we couldn't have any more children, I knew I could face another day because you were there for me. I wanted you to be a success. Because I believed that your success was also a reflection of me."

"It is."

"No, it isn't, Justin. This has been about you for a long time, and I accepted that, but we also agreed that I'd have my turn. Why did I have to leave you in order for our lives to become more fair?"

"I don't feel as if any of this is fair. I want my wife back. I want my partner. We were a team, Cheryl, and I expected your support."

Life was all about Justin.

"Justin, did you know I'm fifty pages short of completing my dissertation to become a doctor of history?"

"What! That's not true."

"Well . . ." She swallowed, her gaze returning to the screen and the squalid conditions two sisters with AIDS lived in. Cheryl paused the movie. "I've never been a liar before."

"Whoa." He backpedaled. "Wait. I didn't say that. I knew you'd been working on it, uh, two, no, three years ago? Right? But I didn't know you were that close. Why didn't I know this?"

"You'd just been appointed ambassador. You left for Ecuador and I stayed in Atlanta with Jett so he could complete his sophomore year of high school. During that time I finished the bulk of the work."

"Still that's a huge time commitment. How did you get everything accomplished?"

"I worked lots of late nights. I took online classes, and the work-study program at Georgia State is amazing."

"So that's why you didn't want to come with me to Ecuador right away."

Cheryl laughed through his stinging selfishness. "No, darlin'," she said, the ache consuming her. "*We decided* not to move Jett in the middle of the school year. I promise, I didn't stay in Atlanta so I could sneak around behind your back and get my doctorate degree."

"I never said that," he retorted. To Cheryl he sounded lost. The light had been cut on, but Justin was still eclipsed by the size of his own ego. Cheryl blamed herself for aiding and abetting his self-directed ardor.

"Why didn't you ever finish?"

She shook her head. "I guess I got busy."

"Do you blame me?" he asked quietly.

Cheryl sighed. "No, that would be too easy. I don't blame anyone."

"You're not being honest. Why haven't you finished? There's a reason."

"I didn't finish because . . ." Cheryl hated the insecure woman she'd been. "I convinced myself that my present life was enough. I didn't want to compete with you, but now I realize I was wrong. Teaching is what I was meant to do."

"Your grades good?" he asked and she wondered why.

"Dean's list."

"Wow. My wife is smart."

I've been smart all along, she wanted to say but didn't. Why did it take her leaving before he discovered her qualities were of more intrinsic value than just meal planning?

She waited for him to retract the sarcastic comment, but he didn't. The ache inside her exploded, and the want she'd had for him seeped away.

"I've got to go." She pressed the PLAY button on the remote. The voices of the women filled the room.

"Why? We were having such a good conversation. Come home, Cheryl. We can work this out. We can talk some more. *Black Enterprise* magazine arrived last week."

"I saw the newspaper this morning," she cut in.

"Tomorrow, you're going to Macon, Savannah, Jonesboro, and East Point. I think you're still running for the Senate, right?"

"Of course."

A sob made her catch her breath. "Okay then. Bye."

"Cheryl, wait."

She could hear her husband's voice, but Cheryl pressed the button until the phone went black.

Cradling her face, she let her tears slide off her fingertips. Justin wasn't ever going to change.

The door to the screening room opened and she strained to see. Cheryl rummaged in her purse for a handkerchief. "This room is occupied," she called into the darkness.

"Mind if I join you?"

"Chad?" she said, her heart thumping wildly.

"The one and only."

"Now isn't a good time."

Instead of leaving, Chad walked down the ramp and to the front of the ten-row room.

She dug in her purse frantically. "Please go away."

"Why?"

She found the soft kerchief and dabbed at her eyes as she stood. "I need to be alone."

"I think you need a friend."

"Justin," she said, exasperated. "Don't think for me. I know what I want. I know what I need."

"My name is Chad. You want to try that again? And if you must tell me off, stick to what I've done wrong to you."

Cheryl took in a big breath and wound up

speechless. "I'm sorry. We had a disagreement. I—"

Chad got a little closer, opened his arms, and enveloped her. "You don't have to explain."

The easy comfort Cheryl had come to know as Chad slid through her system, and as languid as a flowing stream she lifted her arms and embraced him.

His solace quieted her frustration, until the tears stopped, leaving two adults and the stirrings of something else.

Cheryl wondered what that said about her, that she'd just been arguing with her husband and, minutes later, accepting comfort from another man.

Was she seeking a replacement? Did she know in her heart that she and Justin were no more?

Cheryl didn't know. All she knew was that Chad wasn't complicated, and he wasn't deceitful. She knew that her curves fit into his build and she knew how easy it would be for her to lift her mouth to his and ask for a kiss.

Move, her brain instructed in that stern manner she'd come to know was a protective mechanism.

Cheryl released the pressure of her hands on his back, her chest from his chest, her cheek from his. Yet even as she slid from his embrace, he never fully let her go.

"This segment of the film is sad as hell. Why don't you skip to the next one?" he said.

Cheryl tried to regain her equilibrium. "How would you know?"

His eyebrow raised as he turned to the images

of the sick women flickering on the screen. "Are you the only academic mind that can appreciate a good documentary?"

"No." She backed away, her hands operating with minds of their own as she sat down and reached for him. Cheryl withdrew her hand quickly.

"Lady," he practically crooned, as he lifted the armrest between the two seats, "don't mind if I do." He sat next to her, her hand secure in the heart of his.

Holding hands felt odd, she hadn't done it in so long. Ambassadors didn't hold their wives' hands. It implied intimacy, something politicians only seemed to want to have with the public— during an election year.

But this was Chad. And Cheryl knew how he felt about her. Holding hands was a precursor to acts best done in a bedroom. And she wasn't going there.

"We're in a private theater, where we can't be disturbed by anyone, watching a movie that is surprisingly good, if I may say so, holding hands. What's the worst that can happen?" Chad asked her. Looking good, smelling even better.

"Nothing," she answered softly.

"Then why are you squeezing the hell out of my fingers?"

A surprising burst of laughter shot out of her mouth, easing her guilty conscience. "I can hold my own hand, thank you," she said and tried to regain her digits.

To Cheryl's surprise, he folded her hand around his biceps. "I like it there."

Their faces were mere inches apart and she realized he was educating her in the school of Chad. He liked being in the dark, watching a documentary about South Africa, with her.

"That could get uncomfortable," she said.

"Not if we were this way."

Before Cheryl could fully comprehend what happened, she was on her back with Chad over her.

Both of her hands were on his biceps.

"This could only get better if you were saying, 'Yes, Chad. Yes, yes, yes.'"

Despite herself, Cheryl smiled. "You're funny."

The viewing room door opened and Cheryl stiffened. She tried to get up, but Chad applied pressure with his forearms and legs. "Shh. They'll go away."

Terrified, Cheryl lay beneath Chad wishing she could dissolve into water and evaporate.

Soon the door closed and the breath eased out of her mouth.

They remained quiet.

"I'll make a prediction," he said.

"What is that?"

"One day we'll be this way," he said, as his impressive length pressed into her.

Although her stomach fluttered, and she could feel his pulse quicken, she didn't want to get his hopes up. What she was doing was wrong. "Life isn't just about that."

"You're right, but if everything else is rockin' and you add some good lovin', life doesn't get much better than that."

Cheryl had to agree, but she didn't say so.

"Come on," he said, giving her a hand up to a sitting position. "Before we get into trouble."

They watched the rest of the movie, and he pointed to the credits. "Hmm, I wonder who that is."

"Chad Brown. Oh, my goodness. You made this documentary?"

"Why'd you think I recommended it?"

He wore a big grin, but she could see he was ready to burst.

"It was amazing. I'm so impressed." Cheryl gathered her papers and purse and boxed the remaining DVDs. She started up the ramp, the overhead EXIT sign the only light on.

"Well, thank you."

"I wish I could have seen them all," she said. "But another time. You obviously spent a lot of time over there. Maybe you could steer me in the direction of some more reading material."

Chad moved slowly toward her and Cheryl moved too, until her side was pressed into the wall. She thought about turning, but either way, he'd hit an erogenous zone. She had to stay where she was. "What are you doing?" she whispered.

"Asking for a kiss."

"No," she said, her heart galloping.

"Can I have a French kiss then? There's a difference."

He sounded so sexy she almost didn't refuse. He'd asked when they were in Ecuador, but she'd flatly refused. Her refusal seemed to cool his ardor, but apparently not enough. Today, she

wanted to feel wanted. This time she hesitated.
"No."

"Your neck?"

"Chad," she cajoled.

"Your ass?"

She gasped.

"You need a little encouragement."

His chest pressed on her shoulder and his arms
became anchors on the wall by her head. Cheryl
knew if she was face-to-face with Chad, she'd kiss
him.

So she turned slightly and he walked her face-
first into the wall. With her cheek against the
cool paint and Chad's body full-length against
her backside, she couldn't think of anything
more sexy.

"I'm going to kiss something, I probably should
have made that clear. You're running out of
choices before I try out a few and see what I like
best."

Cheryl couldn't think straight. Didn't want to
consider the consequences. She just wanted a
taste. "French kiss," she said, her voice husky
even to her own ears.

Chad didn't turn her around as she thought he
would. He claimed her mouth just as she was,
playing on her vulnerability just enough to make
her open for him.

He laved her tongue, rolling it between his, his
hand tilting up her head until their mouths
could dance without interruption.

Cheryl tried to ease back, but she stopped
when he braced both hands on her thighs and
drove himself into her from behind.

Cheryl stretched up on her toes, knowing if there were no Hugo Boss and Chanel between them, there'd be no stopping.

These were the kisses she missed.

The kisses she should be having with her husband.

The door to the viewing room opened and her eyes fluttered.

They were ten feet from the door.

"Get out," Chad said, in a tone that brooked no argument.

"He has a camera," she muttered as the whir of the shutter hummed quietly. The door slammed closed and Chad took off after the man.

Cheryl sank to the floor and wept.

Twenty-four

"And if you elect me senator of Georgia," Justin's opponent said to the town hall audience of students, "you will get answers to your questions, a supporter of your initiatives, and a voice in the White House. I won't change parties, and I won't lie to you. Thank you."

Justin waited for the applause to die down.

"Mr. Stevens is a good man," Justin said. "We've served together in one form of government or another for many years, and I'm sure no matter the outcome of this race, making Georgia a better state to this country will always be our priority.

"Let me first ask, where are my high school students?"

Justin walked off stage at the Georgia Tech campus. "Stand up. Get up. I know you can get loud! Come on!"

The young men and women stood up and created an absolute stir. Justin let them get raucous and then waved them down.

"All right, and the rest of you sophisticated young men and women are in college, right? Well, I asked you all here together because it's time to talk about you. What's important to you?

I know your friends asked you why you're wasting a perfectly good afternoon listening to that old guy when you could be studying with them."

They laughed at his mock serious expression. "I want you to know I'm not wasting your time. Most people go to college to get an education in the hopes that they'll get a degree. But after you earn that paper, where will you get a job? And if we take a step back for a minute, and go back to high school, you've got so many people pulling at you to go, do, be all you can, until you think, what is it that *I* want to do with my life?

"Should I go to the service or get a job? The question becomes, where? You see, businesses are closing up in this state at a rate of twenty-five per day. It's startling to see once-thriving communities fall to wastelands because the owners couldn't thrive anymore. When I was seventeen the same thing was going on. The good news is that you are the entrepreneurs of the future. Here sit some of the brightest minds of our country and you are largely ignored, and that should change."

The applause was deafening. "Let me give you some statistics as to how incredible your power is. People between the ages of fifteen and thirty represent sixty-five percent of all new patents. That means within your age group, y'all are patenting ten inventions every six seconds. Faster than businesses are closing, you're inventing new ones. People," he said, inciting them, "you are the employers of tomorrow, and you should have a representative in government that speaks for you."

Applause broke into his speech. But Justin didn't care. He had them eating out of his hand and that's exactly what he wanted.

Justin returned home late, his feet hurting as bad as his back. Voices of all the people he'd met today rang in his head and he just wanted to sit down, put his feet up, caress his wife's back, and forget about everything.

Damn. He no longer had a wife to come home to.

The scent of her perfume was fading from the air, and Justin wondered if he'd one day forget that too.

He opened the refrigerator to answer his rumbling stomach, but found nothing. Not even a piece of fruit or shaved meat that he could put on a Kaiser roll. Cheryl knew how he liked his evening snacks, but she hadn't been home in ten days. And it didn't look like she planned on coming back. His evening snack wasn't important to her anymore.

Justin flicked on the kitchen light and stuck his head inside the pantry. He grabbed a sleeve of crackers, peanut butter, and a liter of Coke and headed to his office. He might as well get comfortable and sleep in there. He hated sleeping without Cheryl there to hug him in the middle of the night. He couldn't awaken to watch her grab the last few winks of sleep before he claimed her body, or for her to call him handsome for no reason at all.

He was home alone and he hated it.

Justin lay on the sofa, his legs up, propped the food on his chest, and unscrewed the top of the jar. Peanut butter used to give him a headache, but he hadn't had it in about ten years. Surely his body had worked out its problem by now.

Using the sterling silver knife Cheryl never let him take out of the kitchen, he stacked peanut butter high on the cracker and popped it into his mouth. His taste buds exploded and he grinned. This stuff was awesome.

Justin flicked on the television, caught an old episode of *The Jeffersons* on "Nick at Nite," and tried to relax.

What was he going to do about Cheryl?

Shaw had called the situation right by having him announce their separation. When reporters asked about his marital status, he made it obvious that he wouldn't entertain questions about his private life and asked for a serious reporter to ask an important question.

He appreciated that the media had for the most part directed their curiosity at him, but he had no idea what Cheryl faced on a daily basis. He did appreciate that she wasn't vindictive. His campaign could be suffering a lot more if she were.

The polls reflected that he was making strides each day, but Justin didn't want to just win, he wanted to win by a landslide.

The house phone rang, and he quickly picked it up. "Justin Crawford."

"I'm sorry. I thought I was leaving a voice mail. Sorry to disturb you."

"No problem. Who is this?" The accent was African, although he couldn't place the region.

"This is Hugh Jumbo, and I am the recruiter who helped facilitate Mrs. Crawford being hired to teach at the University of South Africa. I set up the interview for her in Puerto Rico. Anyway, President Mandeke asked me to call and see if it was possible for Mrs. Crawford to leave Atlanta a week from next Tuesday."

Taken aback, Justin wasn't sure what to say. He licked peanut butter from his gums. "She's not here right now."

"I do apologize. Please forgive the late call. Please have her contact me at her earliest convenience. If she cannot come, we will work something out. We are very excited. Her class has been filled since students could sign up for it. We hope she will agree to offer this class twice this semester. Good evening, Mr. Crawford."

"Good evening," Justin said and hung up. So Cheryl was really going. And he was going to let her. He didn't know if he was ambitious or just crazy. Everything his brothers had said had made sense, except him leaving. Somehow, he couldn't make himself do that.

In his heart he didn't believe they would stay separated. That's how he made it through the long days and longer nights. He wanted to believe their love and history would bring them through.

He dialed Shaw. "We need to kick this up a level."

"Right now?" she asked, for the first time sounding as if she was asleep.

"Now would be good, but we can wait until daylight."

"Why aren't you resting?"

"I can't sleep. I want to debate again. Can you make it happen for Monday?"

"No, we don't have the financial resources to pay for more TV time. Let the TV spots we're already running do their job. You're booked on ten radio shows next week. We've got daily promos of you in different venues that will be posted on the Web site. Every day until the election, you've got five question chat-with sessions scheduled with every newspaper that signed up by midnight yesterday."

"How many were there?"

"Thirty. That will be time-consuming because it's real-time interviews, but necessary since we don't have another debate scheduled."

"What about the campaign funds coming in?"

"We're spending those on security, signage, billboards, transportation, and other expenses I can't think of at this second. If you'd like, I can get my laptop, but I'd rather not."

"Shaw, are you sleepy?" he asked, surprised.

"No, sir. I've mastered the art of sleeping standing up, but since I'm not alone, I'd rather not go there in a conversation with you."

"Oh. Well, hell. TMI, Shaw. Good night, and next time don't pick up the phone if you can't talk."

"Yeah, right," she said and hung up.

Justin hung up too, but as soon as he lay the phone down, it rang.

"Crawford," he answered, knowing it was Shaw.

"I know this is touchy given the circumstances, but you've got several academic appearances next week."

"And?"

"It would be nice, since your wife is going to be teaching in Africa, to have her with you. Just a thought. She's already made her decision to go, I know and understand. Even if she can't make the appearances, it would be nice to have her at your victory party."

"I hadn't considered that."

"Senator, if you go to Washington without a wife at your side, women from across the globe will be moving to the Metroplex to chase you."

Justin chewed on another stacked cracker but wished he hadn't. His stomach had started to boil. "I'm sure that's an exaggeration."

"I've been there, I know what I'm talking about. Just think about asking her. Good night for the last time."

Justin disconnected and got up. Maybe if he asked Cheryl . . . she'd agree. Especially if it involved students.

Sweat covered his upper lip and his stomach revolted. What the hell was happening to him? He raced for the bathroom. He dumped the peanut butter and crackers in the trash, dialed his wife, and let the phone ring.

So what if it was one in the morning? He needed help.

"Justin?" she answered. "What's wrong?"

"My stomach hurts."

He could hear her rustling in bed. "And what would you like me to do about that?"

"Tell me if I'm allergic to peanut butter."

"Not so much allergic as it doesn't like you."

He crawled onto the couch and lay down.

"Do I have medicine for this?"

She giggled and his heart leaped. "No, because I'd never feed you peanut butter."

"Then why is the pantry full of it?"

"Jett and I can eat peanut butter without a problem."

"That's why I need you, Cheryl. I'll kill myself all alone, and I won't even intend to."

This time she chuckled outright. "I miss you, too."

The words were music to his ear. "Probably not as much as I miss you."

She didn't say anything and Justin wanted her to. "Cheryl, please come home."

"I can't. Just like you can't not be a senator. I can't come home and be the person you want. I'm not that woman anymore."

"Who are you then?"

"A woman who allowed her life to be overtaken by her husband's dreams. Even though she loved him. Now she's willing to risk everything to realize her dream."

"You could dream locally," he suggested, his stomach still churning the gooey mess.

"Just as you could dream internationally." They lapsed into silence. "Are you afraid?" she asked.

This was the first time anyone had asked him how he felt. Before, he'd been wrong for wanting to pursue his dream. But somehow Cheryl understood.

"Yes. I'm afraid I'm losing you. That I've already lost you."

"You could turn this around anytime before I leave."

"And lose everything. I guess in that regard, we both feel the same." Justin grabbed one of her fancy pillows and held it against his stomach. "Come home, Cheryl. I don't know how else to say it. I still love you. Even if you—"

"What, Justin?"

"Have you been with anyone else?"

The silence grew and he could feel his heart ripping to shreds. "Cheryl, how did we get here? Who? Chad?"

"Justin, I haven't been with him in that way. I couldn't. But before it goes there, please, honey, please. Justin?"

"Give me one year, Cheryl. You can go teach in one year. I'll serve out the remainder of Dan's term and I won't run for reelection. I'll go with you to Africa and maybe begin a program to help the sick get international aid."

"Three hundred sixty-five days," she said.

"That's all, I promise."

"Okay," she said. "If it's so easy, give me what you're asking of me. I'll agree to work for one year. Next year we'll come back and you can run for the Senate, presidency, or whatever. I'll complete my doctorate and I'll find a teaching job nearby."

Justin listened to his wife rework their lives and he knew what he'd asked was wrong. He didn't think he could do what she suggested just as she couldn't abide by his request.

"I had no right," he said to her. "I'm sorry. I can't. And I can't ask you give up your dream."

For the first time in his adult years, he felt like crying. "Cheryl?"

"Yes?" She was crying.

"I need to ask you one more favor. The election is a week from Tuesday. Will you come to the victory party before you board your plane?"

She was really crying and she took in two deep breaths. "Where am I going?"

"Hugh Jumbo called."

She got real quiet. "What did he say?"

"They want you there early. A week from Tuesday."

"That's election night."

"I know." His heart broke that she bothered to know more about his world than he knew about hers. "Will you at least think about it?"

"I don't have to. I'll be there and then I'll go. Take some of the pink stuff for your stomach. Good night, Justin."

The phone died in his ear and Justin put it down. His stomach burned, but the only embers he saw were from the match he'd lit upon their lives.

Sleep eluded him until he just lay there watching the dawn.

As the sun crested the horizon, he knew there was only one right thing to do. He had to let Cheryl go.

Twenty-five

Cheryl dressed slowly, her whole body aching under the effects of her dishonesty. She should have told Justin about kissing Chad, but she couldn't fix her mouth to try to explain why she'd allowed her vows to be compromised. There was no excuse. But there was a logical conclusion. She had to end their "friendship." Her situation with Justin might not ever improve, but she couldn't cross the line between right and wrong.

The hotel phone rang. Only two people knew she was here. "Hello?" she said, hoping it was Keisha.

"Hello, beautiful. How are you this morning?"

Her heart leaped, only to be spanked into submission by guilt. "Chad, we have to talk."

"Good, because I'm in the lobby. Want to have a quick breakfast? Or I can come up?"

"Chad, we can't," she whispered, although she was alone.

"I meant for privacy's sake. I'm a man of my word."

Guilt over her hasty assumption confirmed her

decision. "How about the café downstairs in fifteen minutes? Is that good for you?"

"I'll see you then."

Cheryl let out a frustrated moan, her arms
tight around her stomach. She had to tell Chad
she couldn't see him anymore. And then she had
to be strong enough to leave her husband.

A knock on her door made her head come up
fast. Chad was being persistent and now wasn't
the right time.

She opened the door and Keisha walked in.
"We need to talk."

Cheryl followed, knowing this talk would forever change them. "Would you like some juice? It
was delivered half an hour ago. They promised it
was fresh."

"No, I just want the truth."

Cheryl finished her juice before she sat down
on the sofa.

"What is it?"

"I saw Chad in the café, and I'm concerned that
you're in over your head. I know I'm your sister-in-
law and that we're friends, so I don't want to come
off as if I'm only taking the Crawfords' side. But
nothing good can come from a relationship with
that young man."

Cheryl twirled the glass in her hand. "I know.
I'm ending it today."

Keisha's eyes widened. "What happened between you two?"

"Just a kiss, but I felt it in here." She tapped her
chest. "Deep in there, Keisha, but that's no excuse. While I'm here, I'll respect my vows. My

friendship with Chad is over." Even as she said the words, a part of her wanted to weep.

"And when you're in Africa?"

She looked into Keisha's sad eyes. "If Justin doesn't come with me, then our marriage is over." Cheryl put the glass on the table and stood up. "I've got a meeting so I'd better get going."

"With him?"

"Let's not go there. Give my best to Julian."

Cheryl picked up her purse and her briefcase, kissed her sister-in-law on the cheek, and left the room.

The pictures the photographer had taken of Cheryl and Chad were misleading and graphic. They told a story of pure, unadulterated passion between two people where age and decorum didn't have a place.

"How much did these cost you?" she asked him. Cheryl's eyes stayed riveted to the images. He had photos of them when Chad had lain her on the seats in his brazen effort to seduce her. Had Chad insisted she could have been his, but she'd stopped him.

In the photos her eyes were glazed, her lips parted, her head thrown to the side, her hands splayed against the wall. She looked wanton. But one photo stood out. Right before their lips met, his gaze seemed to ask permission and hers answered. The photographer shooting them captured her hesitancy and in the next shot her agreement.

Her tender expression showed her love for him.

Cheryl was shocked at what one photo could show, but life said she should love only one man and that was the man she was married to.

"Tell me the price," Cheryl asked again.

"I had the money."

"That's not what I asked you."

"Accept them as my parting gift to you."

She reached into her purse and pulled out her checkbook. Her fingers trembled, making it difficult to remove the check from the register. "I know they must have cost a fortune. I know why he did this to me, but he has no right to ruin your life. You don't deserve this."

Cheryl stopped talking and looked at Chad's expression. Usually he smiled at her. Flirted with her. But now he did neither. His face was so serious, so somber. It was as if he knew the end had arrived.

She tried to swallow the lump in her throat and looked back at her checkbook. She hadn't inserted an amount.

She stuffed the offensive manila envelope into her briefcase to shred later. No one would ever see those pictures again.

"Sweetheart, is this the end?" he asked.

"I can't anymore, Chad. My life is unsteady and sensitive. I feel like I'm scattered emotionally. I should never have started anything with you."

"You didn't start with me," he said defensively. "And I didn't give you much of a choice. So stop feeling guilty for my attraction to you."

Unexpected tears ran down her cheeks. "I

can't live the life of two women. It doesn't matter how I feel about you, Chad. We have to end this."

"It matters to me. For once, be honest."

"Nothing I say is going to matter. Please, tell me how much I owe you so I can go."

"One evening in your arms," he answered, "or twenty thousand dollars."

She blinked, forcing his words into her brain. "Really?" she said quietly.

He dropped a receipt on the table. It was labeled *professional photos.* "I paid forty thousand. Since I was the other proud participant, it's only fair that I pay my share. I was offered the ambassadorship to Ecuador."

She looked up, shocked. "Will you take it?"

"No. I've got another opportunity. Can I come see you?"

"In Africa?"

"If that's where you are."

Cheryl covered her eyes, wishing the words had come from her husband. She wrote the check and handed it to Chad.

"I wish we hadn't come to this moment. I just can't."

He held her hand. "Then tell me the truth. Tell me what's on your heart."

Cheryl flipped over a deposit slip, afraid the words she wanted to say would be overheard by the wrong ears. She wrote, *If I met you at the market in beautiful Johannesburg, I would want to get to know you. If you were who you are now, I'd probably fall in love with you.*

She folded the paper, slid it across the table, and got up.

The café was empty except for the staff who were busy setting up for lunch. No one hurried them.

Chad read the message, folded the paper, and put it in his breast pocket. He paid their check and guided her toward the exit. Suddenly he veered off at a hallway behind a lattice room divider, and pulled her into a dimly lit room. She could see that it was a private meeting room with seating for twelve.

Cheryl started to protest but Chad's pained expression quieted her. Without words he put her briefcase and purse gently on the chair.

When he turned around, he opened his arms.

Cheryl walked into them, and kissed him with bittersweet passion. This was good-bye.

As her tears flowed, he kissed her cheeks and her neck, his strong hands keeping her against him.

Were it not for the restrictions on her life, Cheryl would have given herself to him right then. Mind, body, and soul.

"I love you," he said, and she wished life were different. "I know you won't say you love me." Chad's strained voice was tight with emotion. "Just say okay. So I know you feel me. Just so I know . . ."

With her arms around his neck, she absorbed his strength and whispered, "Okay. Good-bye, Chad."

Cheryl quickly got her things and left the room without looking back.

Twenty-six

For eleven days Justin worked nonstop until he knew he couldn't give another piece of himself to his campaign. He'd crossed the state six times in the past six weeks, and he hoped his efforts would pay off in a big way.

As he dressed for his victory party, he remembered back to the night he'd been at the Hilton to announce his intention to run. His entire family had been present, but that wouldn't be the case tonight.

His leaving Cheryl constituted an act of desertion to his brothers, and of the five, three were hardly speaking to him.

Mom and Dad would always be his parents, but they were disappointed as well. Dinners at their house had been quiet, strained events.

His running for the Senate had fractured a family he never thought could be broken. Justin hoped the people of Georgia appreciated what he'd sacrificed for them. And he hoped his family could one day understand.

Shaw entered the suite and sized him up. "Great suit. Is your son coming?"

"No."

"Why not?"

"He's not speaking to me and I haven't been able to reach him at school."

"What about your wife?"

"I don't think so."

"Yesterday you said you thought she would."

"Now I'm saying I don't think so. Sue me."

"Fine. Plan B is Lea North. She's the right mixture of sexuality and quiet strength, and she's a widow. The public will forgive you for the wife debacle, if they see North's wife supporting you. There is still nothing going on there, right?"

"I finally figured out why I don't like you. You're crass. *The wife debacle?* Is this how my campaign will be chronicled in the annals of history?"

"Don't be so sensitive," she said, his critique rolling off her in waves. "We're almost done. And for your information I've been told I'm crass. But there's nothing I can do about it. This is the way God made me."

Justin Crawford adjusted his tie and went into the powder room to make sure it was knotted properly.

He especially missed Cheryl right now. He hadn't tied a tie in fifteen years. She'd always insisted on tying it for him. She'd stand on the bed and reach around his neck as they watched themselves in the mirror.

He'd lean back and nestle his head between her breasts. Then he'd love to watch her face when the tip of her tongue would jutt from the corner of her mouth. Justin loved to be a distraction to her otherwise precise personality.

When he saw the tip of her tongue, his self-control would unwind and he'd take her soaring to peaks where they'd been a thousand times.

Then they'd start all over again. But that was part of the ritual. Part of their lives.

Shaw came up behind him and brushed lint off his back, and he jumped. "Easy, cowboy. Save your surprise for the cameras."

The doorbell to the suite rang out a melody and Maura, who never liked Shaw, said, "Mr. Crawford, sir, sir, sir, sir."

"Your brothers are here," Shaw told him. "Got your victory speech?"

"Yes, and the other one—"

"Give it to me." She looked annoyed.

Justin handed over the piece of paper.

"Losers always find themselves with too much mic time after they've said their thank-yous. What else is there to say? Winners need speeches. You'll be so excited you won't remember the people who helped get you where you are." She made it sound as if a win was a foregone conclusion. "Tonight, sir, you'll only need one speech. Which would you rather have?"

He patted his breast pocket.

"You've chosen well." Suddenly she froze and her finger went to her ear. "Excellent, Randall," she said to her assistant. "Get her twenty and get back to me stat."

"Whose twenty?" Justin asked.

"Don't get your hopes up, but your wife. She disappeared from sight, so if she's still here we'll have her prepped and ready ASAP." Shaw glanced over to the rest of the Crawford men. "Egads. You're all gorgeous."

Justin couldn't help the jolt of surprise. Shaw had never so much as blinked at a man in his presence. "I didn't know there was a female inside your skin."

"Glad I could clarify my anatomy for you. Everyone, pay attention. Where are your wives?"

"They had a Cheryl sighting too," Julian said. "Why aren't the televisions on?"

"Because they can psyche a candidate out. I don't ever turn them on until ten o'clock. That way the candidate isn't tortured. Trust me, we're on top of things."

Justin walked over to his brothers and shook their hands. Win or lose, they were still family. "Glad you came," he said, wishing he could reassure them he was doing the right thing. There was a hole in his heart, but he didn't know how big it would get until after he saw his wife.

"You might not have done this the way we wanted, but we're still family," Nick said, his eyes piercing Justin's for answers.

No one would understand his decision. But he and Cheryl had something special. If he died right now, he'd die knowing he'd been loved by the best woman in the world.

His parents and sisters-in-law converged upon the room, children of all ages in tow. Julian had the biggest brood, followed by Edwin. Hanging on to Terra were two children that he didn't recognize.

He watched as Michael tried to coax the little one out of Terra's arms with a piece of cheese.

Justin had to laugh. The kid was smart. He grabbed a cracker, took it with him, and let the little girl see him hand it to Terra. "Who do we have here?"

"This is Cynthia and Falondra. My sister's children. They're staying with us for a while. Girls, say hello to your new uncle Justin."

The tiny one who was all of about three drew away, but took the cracker.

Michael grimaced. "Lucky guess."

The older girl, who looked about five, gazed up at him. Justin got the distinct impression he was being sized up, so he stooped down and met her steady gaze.

"If you become president, can we sleep over at your house?"

Several family members chuckled. "You'll be my very first sleepover."

She slipped behind Terra's dress, suddenly shy. "T-T, he said we could sleep over his house."

"I know, sweetie. Let's get something to eat."

"You still have a way with the women," Julian said, and eyed his watch.

"Thanks. You still angry with me?"

"It's your life. I was only trying to stop you from screwing it up."

"Why are you so sure I am?"

"Because of these." He handed Justin a packet of papers. "Michael doesn't realize that I know everything that goes on in our law offices."

Somberly, Justin pushed the packet of divorce papers into his breast pocket. "I'm not going to be selfish anymore."

Televisions around the room flickered on and

suddenly everyone's attention was riveted to the close race he and John Stevens were in.

"The polls closed in DeKalb County, Georgia, two hours ago and with forty percent of the precincts in, Justin Crawford has just gained a nice lead . . ."

His family cheered and Justin, who'd tried to stay on the periphery, couldn't fight the feeling. This was his night, and he wanted to enjoy every minute.

Cheryl left the confines of the hired car, the Hilton looming large above her. Ever since the World Trade Center tragedy, she'd always felt a sense of reluctance at entering tall buildings, but tonight she didn't want to be afraid of anything. Not terrorism, or fate.

She wanted to wish Justin well and see her family again for what might be a long time.

She entered the grand ballroom and took in the moment unnoticed. The room was tasteful, the band impeccable, the ambiance perfect. She couldn't have done better herself.

People milled about with cups of nonalcoholic punch, but the majority of the crowd huddled in front of televisions, with smatterings of cheers for Justin. He was winning, by the landslide she knew was fitting for him. She searched out familiar faces, but saw none. The Crawfords were probably sequestered somewhere in the hotel.

She'd intentionally removed herself from the family—his family—these past few weeks, so she didn't know the inside happenings anymore.

The decision hadn't been easy, but necessary, as she had to follow her dream or wither into a woman she didn't want to know.

Cheryl considered locating the family, but decided instead to be one of his fans, for the last time.

As she watched the growing crowd, she wondered how she could have asked him to leave all of this.

Being a leader was his life. And by marrying him, she'd etched hers next to his.

Justin had followed his destiny. She was the one who'd created a fork in their road and followed it.

She only had thirty minutes. If she missed Justin, she could at least say she'd tried to be there for him until the end.

A low roar grew and Cheryl turned toward it.

Her breath came in sharply as Justin and the family entered the ballroom and took the stage. Six of the most handsome men the world had ever seen looked out over the crowd like warriors, and Cheryl smiled with pride. The applause was deafening.

Justin stepped out, front and center. And the cheers echoed through her until she knew she'd never forget this moment. This was the way it was supposed to be.

The final thread of hope broke, but instead of plummeting, Cheryl felt lighter.

Shaw took the microphone. "Ladies and gentlemen, I present to you the next senator for the state of Georgia, Justin Thurgood Crawford!"

In the midst of all the accolades, Cheryl met

her husband's gaze and she smiled from her heart. She didn't realize she'd pressed her hands to her lips until she blew him a kiss, releasing him.

Cheryl turned and was nearly at the door when he began to speak.

"Ladies and gentlemen," he said, "I'm honored to address you as Senator-elect Justin Thurgood Crawford. I wouldn't be here today were it not for support throughout the years from my wife, Cheryl, who is currently on a teaching assignment in Africa with my blessings. The support of my family . . ."

She gave a last look to the family and her husband, and walked out of the hotel and into her new life.

Johannesburg stole Cheryl's heart again as she watched the sun set over the mountains. Large-beaked birds dipped the tree branches, while the voices of children playing in the next row of houses provided a comforting melody.

Cheryl needed the distraction to fight the loneliness that stole under her door at night, keeping her awake, wondering what everyone was doing. But then she'd rise and go teach and she'd know she was exactly where she was supposed to be.

Mail had become a highlight in her day with postcards from Jett and Kathy, who'd decided to take a semester off to travel. And today the letter she'd been waiting for had arrived. She'd been granted her doctorate degree in history.

It was the divorce papers she'd received from

Justin that nearly slid from her lap. She inserted them into the envelope to be mailed back to Atlanta.

She caressed his name on the return label and pressed the envelope to her heart. He still occupied major real estate there. Only time would tell as to how long it would take for her love to abate.

Stored away as part of her other life were the expensive jewelry and the designer suits, and in their place were ankle boots and long skirts to combat the relentless sun. Cheryl fingered the thin strand of pearls around her neck. A girl deserved one luxury.

She wore capris today, as much for the heat as to blend in.

The class system was a way of life in Africa, and the high-class perception people had when she'd arrived was something she tried to balance every day.

Gathering her papers, she strolled into the small house she'd paid handsomely for, as CNN came on the television.

"Senator Crawford, why resign after running for office, accepting the position and spending all the money it took to be where you are?"

"My priorities were in the wrong place. I was wrong to let my family fall apart because of that dream. I love my wife and I love my son and I'm estranged from them because of my selfishness."

"Forgive me, sir, but this is quite a shock," the reporter said. "When did you realize this was a mistake?"

Justin smiled. "I knew before the election, but I didn't want to see the signs. Now I know I can't do this without my wife."

"Do you intend to bring her back from her teaching assignment in Africa?"

Cheryl's heart was in her throat. "Uh-no. My wife wouldn't have it and I wouldn't think of it. I love her and I'll do anything to be with her."

A car started up the road and Cheryl was torn.

The sound was so out of character, she hurried to see which of the single teachers had a guest. She knew it was indecent to spy, but guests were so rare, and when someone had company, everyone tended to get excited.

She took up her new post as a voyeur, watching through the screened door. As the car neared, she wondered where it was going. Perhaps the driver was looking for a place to turn around. Nobody lived on this end except her.

Her heartbeat quickened as the approaching car slowed, kicking up dust.

The corners of her mouth lifted as she gazed out. The vehicle stopped in front of her house and the door opened.

Cheryl let go of the mail and it smacked her feet.

She stepped onto the porch as he fully came into view.

Her heart beat in her throat. "You're here."

"Because you're here. Can you forgive me?"

Cheryl flew down the stairs and leapt into Justin's arms.

"Yes," she said, covering him with kisses from her heart. He returned her affection without hesitating, and she loved him for it. The other teachers began to playfully scold her as they applauded.

"I don't care," she said, wrapping her legs around his waist, her arms around his neck as her softened kisses made promises she intended to keep.

Justin's arms around her felt right. She looked into eyes that adored her and felt the same. "I'm in love and I don't care who knows," she said to him.

"Then kiss me." He started up the stairs with her wrapped around him.

Cheryl did as he requested, knowing she'd never get tired, loving the fact that he wouldn't either.

Dear Readers,

I hope you enjoyed KISSED. If you haven't already experienced the Crawfords and want to read more of this wonderful family, you can start the series at the beginning with SILKEN LOVE, KEEPING SECRETS, ENDLESS LOVE and DOCTOR, DOCTOR. I'd love to hear from you, so please email me at carmengreen1201@yahoo.com, or write to me at P.O. Box 956455 Duluth, GA 30096-9508.

Blessings,
Carmen Green

ABOUT THE AUTHOR

CARMEN GREEN began her writing career in 1994, when Kensington Publishing Corporation published her first novel, NOW OR NEVER. Since 1994, more than twenty novels and novellas have been penned by Ms. Green. In 1998, her novel KEEPING SECRETS, made *Emerge Magazine*'s bestsellers list, and in 2001, her novel COMMITMENTS was adapted into a BET TV movie. In 2003, her first women's fiction novel ATLANTA LIVE was published by BET Sepia, and was later voted in the top ten for Romance-Writers of America's best novels for 2003.

Carmen is proud that two new novels will be in stores in 2004. Look for her mainstream novel, DATE NIGHT in September, and this Crawford romance, KISSED, by Kensington Dafina in November.

Carmen is the mother of three, works full time as a health information manager for a medical practice, as she continues to expand her writing career. In her rare moments of free time, she enjoys reading, exercising and traveling.

Grab These Other
Dafina Novels
(mass market editions)

Check Out These Other
Dafina Novels

Look For These Other
Dafina Novels

If I Could   by Donna Hill
0-7582-0131-1   **$6.99**US/**$9.99**CAN

Thunderland   by Brandon Massey
0-7582-0247-4   **$6.99**US/**$9.99**CAN

June In Winter   by Pat Phillips
0-7582-0375-6   **$6.99**US/**$9.99**CAN

Yo Yo Love   by Daaimah S. Poole
0-7582-0239-3   **$6.99**US/**$9.99**CAN

When Twilight Comes   by Gwynne Forster
0-7582-0033-1   **$6.99**US/**$9.99**CAN

It's A Thin Line   by Kimberla Lawson Roby
0-7582-0354-3   **$6.99**US/**$9.99**CAN

Perfect Timing   by Brenda Jackson
0-7582-0029-3   **$6.99**US/**$9.99**CAN

Never Again Once More   by Mary B. Morrison
0-7582-0021-8   **$6.99**US/**$8.99**CAN

Available Wherever Books Are Sold!

Check out our website at www.kensingtonbooks.com.